14-22

ROBERT HICHENS

The Green Carnation

with an introduction by WILLIAM GAUNT

Dover Publications, Inc., New York

This Dover edition, first published in 1970, is an unabridged republication of the work originally published anonymously in London by William Heinemann in 1894. A new introduction has been written especially for this edition by William Gaunt.

Standard Book Number: 486-22223-3
Library of Congress Catalog Card Number: 69-18207

Manufactured in the United States of America
Dover Publications, Inc.
180 Varick Street
New York, N. Y. 10014

Introduction to the Dover Edition

First published without the author's name in September, 1894, *The Green Carnation* won instant success on both sides of the Atlantic by its lighthearted rendering of the exotic style and "decadent" pose of the *fin de siècle* and remains a little masterpiece of literary mimicry and a document of the period that reads today as entertainingly as ever. A reprint was called for before the year 1894 was out, and the author, whose name was then added to the title page, was revealed as a quite young man unknown until then to fame.

He was Robert Smythe Hichens, born in 1864 at the rectory of an English village, Speldhurst in Kent, where his father was clergyman. The Hichens family had a stockbroking ancestry, and the unworldly cleric inherited a fortune that enabled him to indulge his son's taste for music and letters. But Robert Hichens was determined to make his own way. He went to a school of journalism for a year and in his twenties began to earn a modest living by articles and short stories.

Later on he was to make a fortune for himself by his melodramatic novel, *The Garden of Allah*, destined to sell a million copies, to run through endless editions, to be a smash hit when put on the stage, to be three times made into films, first in the silent days and then as a talkie in colour. But this bonanza was ten years in the future when the ambitious journalist of twenty-nine applied himself to a project of a very different kind. How he came to write *The Green Carnation*, as described in his introduction to a new edition published in 1949, a year before his death—and in more detail in his autobiography of 1947, *Yesterday*—is a fascinating story.

After a severe illness he had been urged to go to Egypt for convalescence. He journeyed along the Nile to Luxor and stayed at the fashionable Luxor Hotel. It was crowded with aristocratic and otherwise distinguished English visitors, among whom he made acquaintances. One of them was E. F. Benson, whose account of the social scene in his novel *Dodo*, with its brilliant heroine—drawn, it was supposed, from Margot Tennant, later the Countess of Oxford and

Asquith—was the current talk of London. Another was Reginald Turner, a relative of the newspaper proprietor Lord Burnham and an amusing conversationalist. And a third, Lord Alfred Douglas, "a young man, indeed almost a boy, fair, aristocratic, even poetic looking." Hichens fell into the spirit of their symposia of wit. The cleverness of Benson inspired a desire to emulate him in a study of contemporary society. He listened with eagerness also to what Lord Alfred had to say of his famous friend, Mr. Oscar Wilde.

He had seen Wilde from a distance, lecturing at the Victoria Rooms, Clifton, in London answering to the call of "Author" on the opening night of *Lady Windermere's Fan* while nonchalantly smoking a gold-tipped cigarette, but the idea of actually meeting him, as Lord Alfred Douglas now proposed, was more than Hichens had dared to entertain. Yet true to his promise Lord Alfred arranged it when they were back in England. They met over luncheon, inevitably at London's festive centre of art and intellect, the Café Royal, where Wilde was accustomed to hold court. Another occasion was a convivial party which included the witty Reginald Turner and the young Max Beerbohm, not long down from Oxford. Wilde dropped in one evening at Hichens's rooms for a quiet talk about books. The idea of Hichens's own book, first planted in his mind at Luxor, was sprouting the while. Lord Alfred and Wilde were to be his models. The sight of Oscar one evening in a theatre box with a large carnation dyed bright green in his buttonhole, in the company of five youths all similarly decorated, gave him a title. He set to work at once. The writing came easily and the book was finished in four weeks.

The year 1894 was a high point of aesthetic excitement. John Lane published Wilde's *Salome* (refused a stage licence by the Lord Chancellor two years before), in the translation from the French version made by Lord Alfred Douglas, to whom it was dedicated. Its effect was heightened by the drawings of Aubrey Beardsley, whose genius was at the same time giving its stamp of strange originality to *The Yellow Book*. Max Beerbohm, aged twenty-two, was writing the essays of an exquisite preciosity that were soon to appear as his collected *Works*. It was a flourishing year of "the new dandyism," "the new urbanity," the *bon mot*, the fine phrase—and the fine art of shocking.

Hichens had done his aesthetic homework well. He touched off reminiscent fireworks of paradox and epigram. Wilde might have

said, like his counterpart Esmé Amarinth, "How splendid to die
with a paradox upon one's lips!" He made gleeful variants on the
theme of the vices of virtue and the virtues of vice. He echoed the
remarks on the superiority of art to nature which Wilde borrowed
from Whistler. When Mr. Amarinth, annoyed by a sunset, pauses in
an oration to say, "That sky is becoming so terribly imitative that I
can hardly go on. Why are modern sunsets so intolerably true to
Turner?" he paraphrases Vivian in Wilde's *The Decay of Lying*
who denounced a sunset he was invited to admire as "simply a very
second-rate Turner, a Turner of a bad period." Some passages are
extremely skilful pastiches of the style of *Dorian Gray*. There are
undertones of Pater to give a final touch of aesthetic completeness.
Of action there is none in *The Green Carnation*, save the move from
the sophistication of town to what the characters consider the delicious absurdities of the country. The stream of conversation is the
book.

Oscar Wilde and Lord Alfred Douglas were promptly recognised
in Esmé Amarinth and his young friend, Lord Reginald Hastings.
Hichens's work was a sensation on this score. That it was anonymous
aroused much curiosity. The publisher, William Heinemann, had
shrewdly advised it should be so. "It will be attributed to half the
well-known authors in England," he said, "and sales will soar."
Journalists began a guessing game. Was it by Wilde himself? Or
perhaps Marie Corelli, who had written *The Silver Domino* anonymously? With less probability still, Alfred Austin, later poet laure-
ate, was by some thought responsible.

Wilde and Lord Alfred were not long in doubt either about the
author or whom he meant to portray. As it turned out they were not
offended, though Wilde does not seem to have thought much of the
book. Both, the author records, sent telegrams to the effect that "all
was discovered" and that Hichens had better go into hiding, but
these were jocose. Lord Alfred soon after amiably invited him to dine
and complacently introduced him as the author to inquirers they
encountered.

When *The Green Carnation* first appeared, a critic called it "the
most impudent book ever written." This pronouncement (which, as
might be expected, deterred no one from reading it) draws attention
to one of the ironies involved. If impudent at all, it was to the
critics and a number of respectable personalities of the time outside
the aesthetic sphere. It was not a novel seamed with clues to real but

concealed identities, apart from its two principal characters. The women who appear in it suggest actors in a stage comedy by Wilde rather than actual persons of the day. But there are numerous flippant remarks at the expense of living celebrities mentioned by name, as for instance the women novelists Mrs. Lynn Linton, Rhoda Broughton and Mrs. Humphry Ward, the leviathan of Victorian journalism George Augustus Sala, the actor-manager Sir George Alexander, the actor and dramatist Wilson Barrett, the popular preacher Mr. Haweis (of whom Mrs. Windsor observes that he is "quite a clergyman except when he is in the pulpit of course") —and several more. George Moore did not escape, and on him Mr. Amarinth is especially severe.

Some were annoyed—Mrs. Linton wrote a scathing article on Hichens's presumption, entitled *Young Dogs*. He had some difficulty in convincing those who complained that the derisive comments were in character with those who made them and did not represent his personal opinions.

They were not the main targets of what Holbrook Jackson, in his celebrated work *The Eighteen Nineties*, terms "the most notable satire of its period." The word "satire" implies ridicule and even a certain animus. It raises the question whether Hichens was anti-Wilde and anti-Douglas. At one time I assumed this to be so but rereading brought into view the appreciative aspect of the parody. He sees the amusingness of the aesthetic situation but there is a sympathetic relish in the fun which seems to distinguish it from such earlier satires on the Aesthetic Movement and its promoters as W. H. Mallock's *The New Republic* and W. S. Gilbert's opera *Patience*. A "skit" was Hichens's own milder word for *The Green Carnation*.

Yet the fun was already in fact being shadowed by the gathering storm. The Marquess of Queensberry and his son Lord Alfred Douglas were at odds early in 1894 about the latter's friendship with Wilde. In April, Lord Alfred sent his insulting telegram in answer to the Marquess's protests, "What a funny little man you are." Hichens was surprisingly prompt in giving a version of the incident. Reggie Hastings in *The Green Carnation* sends a telegram in the same wording to his angry father. The reader is left to surmise whether Hichens realized its full implication. In June the irate Marquess called on Wilde in Tite Street, Chelsea, to accuse him of being the corrupter of his son. It was against a sultry background that

Hichens's "skit" appeared in September, and in unpleasant relation with the grim sequence of events in the following year.

In 1895 came Wilde's action against Queensberry for libel, the collapse of the prosecution, Wilde's arrest "on the charge of committing acts of gross indecency with other male persons" and his sentence to two years' imprisonment with hard labour. In the circumstances, lighthearted parody could be made to appear a work of denigration. The entertainment of *The Green Carnation* had acquired a bitter taste. After consultation with his publisher, Hichens, very properly as may be thought, decided to withdraw the book from circulation.

He later recorded the admiring impression he had formed of Wilde on their brief social acquaintance, though afterwards he never saw him again. He occasionally met Douglas and not long before Douglas's death in 1945 had some friendly correspondence with him. But he did not think of republishing *The Green Carnation* until after the Second World War when it was pointed out to him that his work had become a part of literary history. It appears in the present Dover edition at a time when interest in the imaginative and intellectual activities of the nineties is renewed. The freedom of art and expression was the underlying issue in the reaction of the period against the weighty conventions of Queen Victoria's reign. A *jeu d'esprit* such as *The Green Carnation* cannot tell us all about the aims and problems, the relations and encounters of art and moral and social responsibility. But it conveys much of the spirit of the age in a vivid way of its own.

WILLIAM GAUNT

London, 1969

E slipped a green carnation into his evening coat, fixed it in its place with a pin, and looked at himself in the glass, the long glass that stood near the window of his London bedroom. The summer evening was so bright that he could see his double clearly, even though it was just upon seven o'clock. There he stood in his favourite and most characteristic attitude, with his left knee slightly bent, and his arms hanging at his sides, gazing, as a woman gazes at herself before she starts for a party. The low and continuous murmur of Piccadilly, like the murmur of a flowing tide on a smooth beach, stole to his ears monotonously, and inclined him insensibly to a certain thoughtfulness. Floating through the curtained window the soft lemon light sparkled on the silver backs of the brushes that lay on the toilet-table, on the dressing-gown of spun silk that hung from a hook behind the door, on the great mass of Gloire de Dijon roses, that dreamed in an ivory-white bowl set on the writing-table of ruddy-brown wood. It caught the gilt of the boy's fair hair and turned it into brightest gold, until, despite the white weariness of his face, the pale fretfulness of his eyes, he looked like some angel in a church window designed by Burne-Jones, some angel a little blasé from the injudicious conduct of its life. He frankly admired himself as he watched his reflection, occasionally changing his pose, presenting himself to himself, now full face, now three-quarters face, leaning backward or forward, advancing one foot in its silk stocking and shining shoe, assuming a variety of interesting expressions. In his own opinion he was very beautiful, and he thought it right to appreciate his own qualities of mind and of body. He hated those fantastic creatures who are humble even in their self-communings, cowards who dare not acknowledge even to themselves how exquisite, how delicately fashioned they are. Quite frankly he told other people that he was very wonderful, quite frankly he avowed it to himself. There is a nobility in fearless truthfulness, is there not? and about the magic of his personality he could never be induced to tell a lie.

It is so interesting to be wonderful, to be young, with pale gilt hair and blue eyes, and a face in which the shadows of fleeting expressions come and go, and a mouth like the mouth of Narcissus. It is so interesting to oneself. Surely one's beauty, one's attractiveness, should be one's own greatest delight. It is only the stupid, and those who still cling to Exeter Hall as to a Rock of Ages, who are afraid, or ashamed, to love themselves, and to express that love, if need be. Reggie Hastings, at least, was not ashamed. The mantelpiece in his sitting-room bore only photographs of himself, and he explained this fact to inquirers by saying that he worshipped beauty. Reggie was very frank. When he could not be witty, he often told the naked truth; and truth, without any clothes on, frequently passes for epigram. It is daring, and so it seems clever. Reggie was considered very clever by his friends, but more clever by himself. He knew that he was great, and he said so often in Society. And Society smiled and murmured that it was a pose. Everything is a pose nowadays, especially genius.

This evening Reggie stood before the mirror till the Sèvres clock on the chimneypiece gently chimed seven. Then he drew out of their tissue paper a pair of lavender gloves, and pressed the electric bell.

"Call me a hansom, Flynn," he said to his valet.

He threw a long buff-coloured overcoat across his arm, and went slowly downstairs. A cab was at the door, and he entered it and told the man to drive to Belgrave Square. As they turned the corner of Half Moon Street into Piccadilly, he leant forward over the wooden apron and lazily surveyed the crowd. Every second cab he passed contained an immaculate man going out to dinner, sitting bolt upright, with a severe expression of countenance, and surveying the world with steady eyes over an unyielding rampart of starched collar. Reggie exchanged nods with various acquaintances. Presently he passed an elderly gentleman with a red face and small side whiskers. The elderly gentleman stared him in the face, and sniffed ostentatiously.

"What a pity my poor father is so plain," Reggie said to himself with a quiet smile. Only that morning he had received a long and vehement diatribe from his parent, showering abuse upon him, and exhorting him to lead a more reputable life. He had replied by wire—

"What a funny little man you are.—Reggie."

The funny little man had evidently received his message.

As his cab drew up for a moment at Hyde Park Corner to allow a stream of pedestrians to cross from the Park, he saw several people pointing him out. Two well-dressed women looked at him and laughed, and he heard one murmur his name to the other. He let his blue eyes rest upon them calmly as they peacocked across to St. George's Hospital, still laughing, and evidently discussing him. He did not know them, but he was accustomed to being known. His life had never been a cautious one. He was too modern to be very reticent, and he liked to be wicked in the eye of the crowd. Secret wickedness held little charm for him. He preferred to preface his failings with an overture on the orchestra, to draw up the curtain, and to act his drama of life to a crowded audience of smart people in the stalls. When they hissed him, he only pitied them, and wondered at their ignorance. His social position kept him in Society, however much Society murmured against him; and, far from fearing scandal, he loved it. He chose his friends partly for their charm, and partly for their bad reputations; and the white flower of a blameless life was much too inartistic to have any attraction for him. He believed that Art showed the way to Nature, and worshipped the abnormal with all the passion of his impure and subtle youth.

"Lord Reginald Hastings," cried Mrs. Windsor's impressive butler, and Reggie entered the big drawing-room in Belgrave Square with the delicate walk that had led certain Philistines to christen him Agag. There were only two ladies present, and one tall and largely built man, with a closely shaved, clever face, and rather rippling brown hair.

"So sweet of you to come, dear Lord Reggie," said Mrs. Windsor, a very pretty woman of the preserved type, with young cheeks and a middle-aged mouth, hair that was scarcely out of its teens, and eyes full of a weary sparkle. "But I knew that Mr. Amarinth would prove a magnet. Let me introduce you to my cousin, Lady Locke— Lord Reginald Hastings."

Reggie bowed to a lady dressed in black, and shook hands affectionately with the big man, whom he addressed as Esmé. Five minutes later dinner was announced, and they sat down at a small oval table covered with pale pink roses.

"The opera to-night is 'Faust,'" said Mrs. Windsor. "Ancona is Valentine, and Melba is Marguerite. I forget who else is singing, but it is one of Harris's combination casts, a constellation of stars."

"The evening stars sang together!" said Mr. Amarinth, in a

gently elaborate voice, and with a sweet smile. "I wonder Harris does not start morning opera; from twelve till three for instance. One could drop in after breakfast at eleven, and one might arrange to have luncheon parties between the acts."

"But surely it would spoil one for the rest of the day," said Lady Locke, a fresh-looking woman of about twenty-eight, with the sort of face that is generally called sensible, calm observant eyes, and a steady and simple manner. "One would be fit for nothing afterwards."

"Quite so," said Mr. Amarinth, with extreme gentleness. "That would be the object of the performance, to unfit one for the duties of the day. How beautiful! What a glorious sight it would be to see a great audience flocking out into the orange-coloured sunshine, each unit of which was thoroughly unfitted for any duties whatsoever. It makes me perpetually sorrowful in London to meet with people doing their duty. I find them everywhere. It is impossible to escape from them. A sense of duty is like some horrible disease. It destroys the tissues of the mind, as certain complaints destroy the tissues of the body. The catechism has a great deal to answer for."

"Ah! now you are laughing at me," said Lady Locke calmly.

"Mr. Amarinth never laughs at any one, Emily," said Mrs. Windsor. "He makes others laugh. I wish I could say clever things. I would rather be able to talk in epigrams, and hear Society repeating what I said, than be the greatest author or artist that ever lived. You are luckier than I, Lord Reggie. I heard a *bon mot* of yours at the Foreign Office last night."

"Indeed. What was it?"

"Er—really I—oh! it was something about life, you know, with a sort of general application, one of your best. It made me smile, not laugh. I always think that is such a test of merit. We smile at wit; we laugh at buffoonery."

"The highest humour often moves me to tears," said Mr. Amarinth musingly. "There is nothing so absolutely pathetic as a really fine paradox. The pun is the clown among jokes, the well-turned paradox is the polished comedian, and the highest comedy verges upon tragedy, just as the keenest edge of tragedy is often tempered by a subtle humour. Our minds are shot with moods as a fabric is shot with colours, and our moods often seem inappropriate. Everything that is true is inappropriate."

Lady Locke ate her salmon calmly. She had not been in London for ten years. Her husband had had a military appointment in the Straits Settlements, and she had been with him. Two years ago he had died at his post of duty, and since then she had been living quietly in a German town. Now she was entering the world again, and it seemed to her odd and altered. She was interested in all she saw and heard. To-night she found herself studying a certain phase of modernity. That it sometimes struck her as maniacal did not detract from its interest. The mad often fascinate the sane.

"I know," said Reggie Hastings, holding his fair head slightly on one side, and crumbling his bread with a soft, white hand—"I know. That is why I laughed at my brother's funeral. My grief expressed itself in that way. People were shocked, of course, but when are they not shocked? There is nothing so touching as the inappropriate. I thought my laughter was very beautiful. Anybody can cry. That was what I felt. I forced my grief beyond tears, and then my relations said that I was heartless."

"But surely tears are the natural expression of sad feelings," said Lady Locke. "We do not weep at a circus or at a pantomime; why should we laugh at a funeral?"

"I think a pantomime is very touching," said Reggie. "The pantaloon is one of the most luridly tragic figures in art or in life. If I were a great actor, I would as soon play the pantaloon as 'King Lear.'"

"Perhaps his mournful possibilities have been increased since I have been out of England," said Lady Locke. "Ten years ago he was merely a shadowy absurdity."

"Oh! he has not changed," said Mr. Amarinth. "That is so wonderful. He never develops at all. He alone understands the beauty of rigidity, the exquisite serenity of the statuesque nature. Men always fall into the absurdity of endeavouring to develop the mind, to push it violently forward in this direction or in that. The mind should be receptive, a harp waiting to catch the winds, a pool ready to be ruffled, not a bustling busybody, for ever trotting about on the pavement looking for a new bun shop. It should not deliberately run to seek sensations, but it should never avoid one; it should never be afraid of one; it should never put one aside from an absurd sense of right and wrong. Every sensation is valuable. Sensations are the details that build up the stories of our lives."

"But if we do not choose our sensations carefully, the stories may be sad, may even end tragically," said Lady Locke.

"Oh! I don't think that matters at all; do you, Mrs. Windsor?" said Reggie. "If we choose carefully, we become deliberate at once; and nothing is so fatal to personality as deliberation. When I am good, it is my mood to be good; when I am what is called wicked, it is my mood to be evil. I never know what I shall be at a particular moment. Sometimes I like to sit at home after dinner and read 'The Dream of Gerontius.' I love lentils and cold water. At other times I must drink absinthe, and hang the night hours with scarlet embroideries. I must have music, and the sins that march to music. There are moments when I desire squalor, sinister, mean surroundings, dreariness and misery. The great unwashed mood is upon me. Then I go out from luxury. The mind has its West End and its Whitechapel. The thoughts sit in the Park sometimes, but sometimes they go slumming. They enter narrow courts and rookeries. They rest in unimaginable dens seeking contrast, and they like the ruffians whom they meet there, and they hate the notion of policemen keeping order. The mind governs the body. I never know how I shall spend an evening till the evening has come. I wait for my mood."

Lady Locke looked at him quite gravely while he was speaking. He always talked with great vivacity, and as if he meant what he was saying. She wondered if he did mean it. Like most other people, she felt the charm that always emanated from him. His face was tired and white, but not wicked, and there was an almost girlish beauty about it. He flushed easily, and was obviously sensitive to impressions. As he spoke now, he seemed to be elucidating some fantastic gospel, giving forth some whimsical revelation; yet she felt that he was talking the most dangerous nonsense, and she rather wanted to say so. Most of her life had been passed among soldiers. Her father had been a general in the Artillery. Her two brothers were serving in India. Her husband had been a bluff and straightforward man of action, full of hard common-sense, and the sterling virtues that so often belong to the martinet. Mr. Amarinth and Lord Reggie were specimens of manhood totally strange to her— until now she had not realised that such people existed. All the opinions which she had hitherto believed herself to hold in common with the rest of sane people, seemed suddenly to become ridiculous in this environment. Her point of view was evidently remarkably different from that attained by her companions. On the whole, she decided not to dispute the doctrine of moods. So she said nothing, and allowed Mrs. Windsor to break in airily—

"Yes, moods are delightful. I have as many as I have dresses, and they cost me nearly as much. I suppose they cost Jimmy a good deal, too," she added, with a desultory pensiveness; "but fortunately he is well off, so it doesn't matter. I never go into the slums, though. It is so tiring, and then there is so much infection. Microbes generally flourish most in shabby places, don't they, Mr. Amarinth? A mood that cost one typhoid or smallpox would be really silly, wouldn't it? Shall we go into the drawing-room, Emily? the carriage will be round directly. Yes; do smoke, Mr. Amarinth. You shall have your coffee in here while we put on our cloaks."

She rustled out of the room with her cousin. When she had gone, Esmé Amarinth lit a gold-tipped cigarette, and leaned back lazily in his chair.

"How tiring women are," he said. "They always let one know that they are trying to be up to the mark. Isn't it so, Reggie?"

"Yes, unless they have convictions which lead them to hate one's mark. Lady Locke has convictions, I should fancy."

"Probably. But she has a great deal besides."

"Comment?"

"Don't you know why Mrs. Windsor specially wanted you to-night?"

"To polish your wit with mine," said the boy, with his pretty, quick smile.

"No, Reggie. Lady Locke has come into an immense fortune lately. They say she has over twenty thousand a year. Mrs. Windsor is trying to do you a good turn. And I dare say she would not be averse to uniting her first cousin with a future marquis."

"H'm!" said Reggie, helping himself to coffee with a rather abstracted air.

"It is a pity I am already married," added Amarinth, sipping his coffee with a deliberate grace. "I am paying for my matrimonial mood now."

"But I thought Mrs. Amarinth lived entirely upon Crosse and Blackwell's potted meats and stale bread," said Reggie seriously.

"Unfortunately that is only a *canard* invented by my dearest enemies."

IM won't be back till very late, I expect," said Mrs. Windsor to her cousin, as they passed through the hall that night about twelve o'clock, after their return from the opera. "I am tired, and cannot go to my parties. Come to my room, Emily, and we will drink some Bovril, and have a talk. I love drinking Bovril in secret. It seems like a vice. And then it is wholesome, and vices always do something to one—make one's nose red, or bring out wrinkles, or spots, or some horror. Two cups of Bovril, Henderson," she added to the butler, in a parenthesis. "Take off your cloak, Emily, and lie down on this sofa. What a pity we can't have a fire. That is the chief charm of the English summer. It nearly always necessitates fires. But to-night it is really warm."

Lady Locke took off her cloak quietly, and laid it down on a chair. She looked fresh and healthy, but rather emotional. She had not been to "Faust" for such a long time, that to-night she had been deeply moved, despite the intercepting chatter of her companions. Mr. Amarinth's epigrams had been especially voluble during the garden scene.

"It has been a delightful evening," she said.

"Do you think so? I thought you would like Lord Reggie."

"I meant the music."

"The music! Oh! I see. Yes, 'Faust' is always nice; a little thread-bare though, now. Old operas are like old bonnets, I always think. They ought to be remodelled, retrimmed from time to time. If we could keep Gounod's melodies now, and get them reharmonised by Saint-Saëns or Bruneau, it would be charming."

"I think it is a mercy something stands still nowadays," said Lady Locke, lying down easily on the sofa, and leaning her dark head against the cushions. "If all the old-fashioned operas and pictures and books were swept away, like the old-fashioned people, we should have no landmarks at all. London is not the same London it was ten years ago."

Mrs. Windsor lifted her eyebrows.

"The same London? I should hope not. Why, Aubrey Beardsley and Mr. Amarinth had not been invented then, and 'The Second Mrs. Tanqueray' had never been written, and women hardly ever smoked, and —"

"And men did not wear green carnations," Lady Locke said.

Mrs. Windsor turned towards her cousin, and lifted her darkened eyebrows to her fair fringe.

"Emily, what do you mean? Ah! here is our Bovril! I feel so delightfully vicious when I drink it, so unconventional! You speak as if you disliked our times."

"I hardly know them yet. I have been a country cousin for ten years, you see. I am quite colonial."

"Poor dear child. How horrid. I suppose you have hardly seen chiffon. It must have been like death. But do you really object to the green carnation?"

"That depends. Is it a badge?"

"How do you mean?"

"I only saw about a dozen in the Opera House to-night, and all the men who wore them looked the same. They had the same walk, or rather waggle, the same coyly conscious expression, the same wavy motion of the head. When they spoke to each other, they called each other by Christian names. Is it a badge of some club or some society, and is Mr. Amarinth their high priest? They all spoke to him, and seemed to revolve round him like satellites around the sun."

"My dear Emily, it is not a badge at all. They wear it merely to be original."

"And can they only be original in a button-hole way? Poor fellows."

"You don't understand. They like to draw attention to themselves."

"By their dress? I thought that was the prerogative of women."

"Really, Emily, you *are* colonial. Men may have women's minds, just as women may have the minds of men."

"I hope not."

"Dear, yes. It is quite common nowadays."

"And has Lord Reginald Hastings got a woman's mind?"

"My dear, he has a very beautiful mind. He is poetic, imaginative, and perfectly fearless."

"That's better."

"He dares do anything. He is not afraid of Society, or of what the clergy and such unfashionable and limited people say. For instance, if he wished to commit what copy-books call a sin, he would commit it, even if Society stood aghast at him. That is what I call having real moral courage."

Lady Locke supped her Bovril methodically.

"I see," she said, rather drily; "he is not afraid to be wicked."

"Not in the least; and how many of us can say as much? Mr. Amarinth is quite right. He declares that goodness is merely another name for cowardice, and that we all have a certain disease of tendencies that inclines us to certain things labelled sins. If we check our tendencies, we drive the disease inwards; but if we sin, we throw it off. Suppressed measles are far more dangerous than measles that come out."

"I see; we are to aim at inducing a violent rash that all the world may stare at."

Her cousin glanced at her for a moment with a tinge of uneasy inquiry. She was not very sharp, although she was very receptive of modern philosophy.

"Well," she said, a little doubtfully, "not quite that, I suppose."

"We are to sin on the house-top and in the street, instead of in the privacy of a room with the door locked. But what will the London County Council say?"

"Oh, they have nothing to do with our class. They only concern themselves with acrobats, and respectable elderly women who are fired from cannons. That is so right. Respectable elderly women do so much harm. Mr. Amarinth said to-night—in the garden scene, if you remember—that prolonged purity wrinkled the mind as much as prolonged impurity wrinkled the face. Nature forces us to choose whether we will spoil our faces with our sins, or our minds with our virtues. How true."

"And how original. This Bovril is very comforting, Betty; as reviving as—an epigram."

"Yes, my cook understands it. That must be so sweet for the Bovril—to be understood! Do you like Lord Reggie?"

"He has a beautiful face. How old is he? Twenty?"

"Oh no, nearly twenty-five. Three years younger than you are. That is all."

"He looks astonishingly young."

"Yes. He says that his sins keep him fresh. A sinner with a young lamb's heart among the full-grown flocks of saints, you know. Such a quaint idea, so original."

"I want you to tell me which is original, Mr. Amarinth or Lord Reggie?"

"Oh! they both are."

"No, they are too much alike. When we meet with the Tweedle-dum and Tweedledee in mind, one of them is always a copy, an echo of the other."

"Do you think so? Well, of course Mr. Amarinth has been original longer than Lord Reggie, because he is nearly twenty years older."

"Then Lord Reggie is the echo. What a pity he is not merely vocal."

"What do you mean, dear?"

"Oh! nothing. And who started the fashion of the green carnation?"

"That was Mr. Amarinth's idea. He calls it the arsenic flower of an exquisite life. He wore it, in the first instance, because it blended so well with the colour of absinthe. Lord Reggie and he are great friends. They are quite inseparable."

"Yes."

"They are both coming down to stay with me in Surrey next week, and I want you to come too. I always spend a week in the country in June, a week of perfect rusticity. It is like a dear little desert in the oasis, you know. We do nothing, and we eat a great deal. Nobody calls upon us, and we call upon no one. We go to a country church on Sunday once, just for the novelty of it; and this year Mr. Amarinth and Lord Reggie are going to have a school treat. Last year they got up a mothers' meeting instead, and Mr. Amarinth read his last essay on 'The Wickedness of Virtue' aloud to the mothers. They so enjoyed it. One of them said to me afterwards, 'I never knew what religion really was before, ma'am.' They are so deliciously simple, you know. I call my stay in the desert 'the Surrey week.' It is such fun. You will come, won't you?"

Lady Locke was laughing almost against her will.

"Is Jim to be there?" she asked, putting the china bowl, that had held her Bovril, down upon the tiny table, covered with absurd silver knickknacks, at her side.

"Dear no. Jim stays in town, and has his annual rowdy-dowdy week. He looks forward to it immensely. Will you come?"

"If I may bring Tommy? I don't like to part from him. I am an old-fashioned mother, and quite fond of my boy."

"But that's not old-fashioned. It is our girls we dislike. We always take the boys everywhere. You must not mind close quarters. We live in a sort of big cottage that I have built near Leith Hill. We walk up the hill nearly every day after lunch. Tommy can play about with the curate's little boys. They all wear spectacles; but I believe they are quite nice-minded, so that will be all right, as you are so particular."

"And do green carnations bloom on the cottage walls?"

"My dear Emily, green carnations never bloom on walls at all. Of course they are dyed. That is why they are original. Mr. Amarinth says Nature will soon begin to imitate them, as she always imitates everything, being naturally uninventive. However, she has not started this summer yet."

"That is lazy of her."

"Yes. Well, good-night, dear. I am so glad you will come. Breakfast in your room at any time you like of course. Will you have tea or hock and seltzer?"

"Tea, please."

They kissed.

III

R. AMARINTH and Lord Reggie did not go to bed so early. After the performance of "Faust" was over they strolled arm in arm towards a certain small club that they much affected, a little house tucked into a corner not far from Covent Garden, with a narrow passage instead of a hall, and a long supper-room filled with tiny tables. They made their way gracefully to their own particular table at the end of the room, where they could converse unheard, and see all that was to be seen. An obsequious waiter—one of the restaurant race that has no native language—relieved them of their coats, and they sat down opposite to each other, mechanically touching their hair to feel if their hats had ruffled its smooth surface.

"What do you think about it, Reggie?" Amarinth said, as they began to discuss their oysters. "Could you commit the madness of matrimony with Lady Locke? You are so wonderful as you are, so complete in yourself, that I scarcely dare to wish it, or anything else for you; and you live so comfortably upon debts, that it might be unwise to risk the possible discomfort of having money. Still, if you ever intend to possess it, you had better not waste time. You know my theory about money?"

"No; what is it, Esmé?"

"I believe that money is gradually becoming extinct, like the Dodo or 'Dodo'. It is vanishing off the face of the earth. Soon we shall have people writing to the papers to say that money has been seen at Richmond, or the man who always announces the premature advent of the cuckoo to his neighbourhood will communicate the fact that one Spring day he heard two capitalists singing in a wood near Esher. One hears now that money is tight—a most vulgar condition to be in by the way; one will hear in the future that money is not. Then we shall barter, offer glass beads for a lunch, or sell our virtue for a good dinner. Do you want money?"

Reggie was eating delicately, with his fair head drooping on one side, and his blue eyes wandering in a fidgety way about the room.

"I suppose I do," he said. "But, as you say, I am afraid of spoiling myself, of altering myself. And yet marriage has not changed you."

"I have not allowed it to. My wife began by trying to influence me, she has ended by trying not to be influenced by me. She is a good woman, Reggie, and wears large hats. Why do good women invariably wear large hats? To show they have large hearts? No, I am unchanged. That is really the secret of my pre-eminence. I never develop. I was born epigrammatic, and my dying remark will be a paradox. How splendid to die with a paradox upon one's lips! Most people depart in a cloud of blessings and farewells, or give up the ghost arranging their affairs like a huckster, or endeavouring to cut somebody off with a shilling. I at least cannot be so vulgar as to do that, for I have not a shilling in the world. Some one told me the other day that the Narcissus Club had failed, and attributed the failure to the fact that it did not go on paying. Nothing does go on paying. I know I don't."

"I hate offering payment to anybody," said Reggie. "Even when I have the money. There is something so sordid about it. To give is beautiful. I said so to my tailor yesterday. He answered, 'I differ from you, sir, *in toto*.' How horrible this spread of education is! We shall have our valets quoting Horace at us soon. I am told there is a Scotch hairdresser in Bond Street who speaks French like a native."

"Of Scotland or France?"

"Oh! France."

"Then he must have a bad pronunciation. A native's pronunciation of his language is invariably incorrect. That is why the average Parisian is totally unintelligible to the intelligent foreigner. All foreigners are intelligent. Ah! here are our devilled kidneys. I suppose you and I are devilled, Reggie. People say we are so wicked. I wish one could feel wicked; but it is only good people who can manage to do that. It is the one prerogative of virtue that I really envy. The saint always feels like a sinner, and the poor sinner, try as he will, can only feel like a saint. The stars are so unjust. These kidneys are delicious. They are as poetic as one of Turner's later sunsets, or as the curving mouth of La Gioconda. How Frederick Wedmore would love them."

Reggie helped himself to a glass of champagne. A bright spot of red had appeared on each of his cheeks, and his blue eyes began to sparkle.

"Are you going to get drunk to-night, Esmé?" he asked. "You are so splendid when you are drunk."

"I have not decided either way. I never do. I let it come if it will. To get drunk deliberately is as foolish as to get sober by accident. Do you know my brother? When he is not tipsy, he is invariably blind sober. I often wonder the police do not run him in."

"Do they ever run any one in? I thought they were always dismissed the force if they did."

"Probably that is so. The expected always happens, and people in authority are very expected. One always knows that they will act in defiance of the law. Laws are made in order that people in authority may not remember them, just as marriages are made in order that the divorce court may not play about idly. Reggie, are you going to make this marriage?"

"I don't know," said the boy, rather fretfully. "Do you want me to?"

"I never want any one to do anything. And I should be delighted to continue not paying for your suppers. Besides, I am afraid that marriage might cause you to develop, and then I should lose you. Marriage is a sort of forcing house. It brings strange sins to fruit, and sometimes strange renunciations. The renunciations of marriage are like white lilies—bloodless, impurely pure, as anæmic as the soul of a virgin, as cold as the face of a corpse. I should be afraid for you to marry, Reggie! So few people have sufficient strength to resist the preposterous claims of orthodoxy. They promise and vow three things—is it three things you promise and vow in matrimony, Reggie?—and they keep their promise. Nothing is so fatal to a personality as the keeping of promises, unless it be telling the truth. To lie finely is an Art, to tell the truth is to act according to Nature, and Nature is the first of Philistines. Nothing on earth is so absolutely middle-class as Nature. She always reminds me of Clement Scott's articles in the *Daily Telegraph*. No, Reggie, do not marry unless you have the strength to be a bad husband."

"I have no intention of being a good one," Reggie said earnestly.

His blue eyes looked strangely poetic under the frosty gleam of the electric light, and his straight pale yellow hair shone like an aureole round the head of some modern saint. He was eating strawberries rather petulantly, as a child eats pills, and his cheeks were now violently flushed. He looked younger than ever, and it was difficult to believe that he was nearly twenty-five.

"I have no intention of being a good one. It is only people without brains who make good husbands. Virtue is generally merely a form of deficiency, just as vice is an assertion of intellect. Shelley showed the poetry that was in his soul more by his treatment of Harriet than by his writing of 'Adonais'; and if Byron had never broken his wife's heart, he would have been forgotten even sooner than he has been. No, Esmé; I shall not make a good husband."

"Lady Locke would make a good wife."

"Yes, it is written in her face. That is the worst of virtues. They show. One cannot conceal them."

"Yes. When I was a boy at school, I remember so well I had a virtue, and I was terribly ashamed of it. I was fond of going to church. I can't tell why. I think it was the music, or the painted windows, or the precentor. He had a face like the face of seven devils, so exquisitely chiselled. He looked as if he were always seeking rest and finding none. He was really a clergyman of some import-ance, the only one I ever met. I was fond of going to church, and I was in agony lest some strange expression should come into my face and tell my horrible secret. I dreaded above all lest my mother should ever get to know it. It would have made her so happy."

"Did she?"

"No, never. The precentor died, and my virtue died with him. But you are quite right, Reggie; a virtue is like a city set upon a hill, it cannot be hid. We can conceal our vices if we care to, for a time at least. We can take our beautiful purple sin like a candle and hide it under a bushel. But a virtue will out. Virtuous people always have odd noses, or holy mouths, or a religious walk. Nothing in the world is so painful as to see a good man masquerading in the com-pany of sinners. He may drink and blaspheme, he may robe himself in scarlet, and dance the *can-can*, but he is always virtuous. The mind of the *moulin rouge* is not his. Wickedness does not sit easily upon him. It looks like a coat that has been paid for."

"Esmé, you are getting drunk!"

"What makes you think so, Reggie?"

"Because you are so brilliant. Go on. The night is growing late. Soon the silver dawn will steal along the river, and touch with radiance those monstrosities upon the Thames Embankment. John Stuart Mill's badly fitting frock-coat will glow like the golden fleece, and the absurd needle of Cleopatra will be barred with scarlet and with orange. The flagstaff in the Victoria Tower will glitter like an angel's ladder, and the murmur of Covent Garden will be as the murmur of the flowing tide. Oh! Esmé, when you are drunk, I could listen to you for ever. Go on—go on!'"

"Remember my epigrams then, dear boy, and repeat them to me to-morrow. I am dining out with Oscar Wilde, and that is only to be done with prayer and fasting. Waiter, open another bottle of champagne, and bring some more strawberries. Yes, it is not easy to be wicked, although stupid people think so. To sin beautifully, as you sin, Reggie, and as I have sinned for years, is one of the most complicated of the arts. There are hardly six people in a century who can master it. Sin has its technique, just as painting has its technique. Sin has its harmonies and its dissonances, as music has its harmonies and its dissonances. The amateur sinner, the mere bungler whom we meet with, alas! so frequently, is perpetually introducing consecutive fifths and octaves into his music, perpetually bringing wrong colour notes into his painting. His sins are daubs or potboilers, not masterpieces that will defy the insidious action of time. To commit a perfect sin is to be great, Reggie, just as to produce a perfect picture, or to compose a perfect symphony, is to be great. Francesco Cenci should have been worshipped instead of murdered. But the world can no more understand the beauty of sin, than it can understand the preface to 'The Egoist,' or the simplicity of 'Sordello.' Sin puzzles it; and all that puzzles the world, frightens the world; for the world is a child, without a child's charm, or a child's innocent blue eyes. How exquisitely coloured these strawberries are, yet if Sargent painted them he would idealise them, would give to them a beauty such as Nature never yet gave to anything. So it is with the artist in sinning. He improves upon the sins that Nature has put, as it were, ready to his hand. He idealises, he invents, he develops. No trouble is too great for him to take, no day is too long for him to work in. The still and black-robed night hours find him toiling to perfect his sin; the weary white dawn, looking into his weary white face through the shimmering window panes, is greeted by a smile that leaps from sleepless eyes. The passion of the creator is upon him. The man who invents a new sin is greater than the man who invents a new religion, Reggie. No Mrs. Humphry Ward can snatch this glory from him. Religions are the Aunt Sallies that men provide for elderly female venturists to throw missiles at and to demolish. What sin that has ever been invented has ever been demolished? There are always new human beings springing into life to commit it, and to find pleasure in it. Reggie, some day I will write a gospel of strange sins, and I will persuade the S.P.C.K. Society to publish it in dull, misty scarlet, powdered with golden devils."

"Oh, Esmé, you are great!"

"How true that is! And how seldom people tell the truths that are worth telling. We ought to choose our truths as carefully as we choose our lies, and to select our virtues with as much thought as we bestow upon the selection of our enemies. Conceit is one of the greatest of the virtues, yet how few people recognise it as a thing to aim at and to strive after. In conceit many a man and woman has found salvation, yet the average person goes on all fours grovelling after modesty. You and I, Reggie, at least have found that salvation. We know ourselves as we are, and understand our own greatness. We do not hoodwink ourselves into the blind belief that we are ordinary men, with the intellects of Cabinet Ministers, or the passions of the proletariat. No, we—Closing time, waiter? How absurd! Why is it forbidden in England to eat strawberries after midnight, or to go to bed at one o'clock in the day? Come, Reggie! It is useless to protest, as Mr. Max Beerbohm once said in his delicious 'Defence of Cosmetics.' Come, the larks will soon be singing in the clear sky above Wardour Street. I am tired of tirades. How sweet and chilly air is! Let us go to Covent Garden. I love the pale, tender green of the cabbage stalks, and the voices of the costermongers are musical in the dawning. Give me your arm, and, as we go, we will talk of Albert Chevalier and of the mimetic art."

IV

URING the few days that elapsed before the advent of the Surrey week, Lady Locke saw a great deal of Lord Reggie, and became a good deal troubled in her mind about him. He was strangely different from all the men and boys whom she had ever known, almost monstrously different, and yet he attracted her. There was something so young about him, and so sensitive, despite the apparent indifference to the opinion of the world, of which he spoke so often, and with such unguarded emphasis. Sometimes she tried to think that he was masquerading, and that a travesty of evil really concealed sound principles, possibly even evangelical tendencies, or a bias towards religious mania. But she was quickly undeceived. Lord Reggie was really as black as he painted himself, or Society told many lies concerning him. Of course Lady Locke heard nothing definite about him. Women seldom do hear much that is definite about men unrelated to them; but all the world agreed in saying that he was a scamp, that he was one of the wildest young men in London, and that he was ruining his career with both hands. Lady Locke hardly knew why she should mind, and yet she did mind. She found herself thinking often of him, and in a queer sort of motherly way that the slight difference in their ages did not certainly justify. After all, he was nearly twenty-five and she was only twenty-eight, but then he looked twenty, and she felt—well, a considerable age. She had married at seventeen. She had travelled, had seen something of rough life, had been in an important position officially owing to her dead husband's military rank. Then, too, she had suffered a bereavement, had seen a strong man, who had been her strong man, die in her arms. Life had given to her more of its realities than of its shams; and it is the realities that mark the passage of the years, and number for us the throbs in the great heart of time. Lady Locke knew that she felt much older than Lord Reggie would feel when he was twenty-eight, if he went on living at least as he was living now.

"Has he a mother?" she asked her cousin, Betty Windsor, one

day as they were driving slowly down the long line of staring faces that fill the Park at five o'clock on warm afternoons in summer.

Mrs. Windsor, who was almost lost in the passion of the gazer, and who was bowing about twice a minute to passing acquaintances, or to friends rigid upon tiny green chairs, gave a quarter of her mind violently to her companion, and answered hurriedly—

"Two, dear, practically."

"Two!"

"Yes. His own mother divorced his father, and the latter has married again. The second Marchioness of Hedfield wrote to Lord Reggie the other day, and said she was prepared to be a second mother to him. So you see he has two. So nice for the dear boy."

"Do you think so? But his own mother—what is she like?"

"I don't know her. Nobody does. She never comes to town or stays in country houses. But I believe she is very tall, and very religious—if you notice, it is generally short, squat people who are atheists—and she lives at Canterbury, where she does a great deal of good among the rich. They say she actually converted one of the canons to a belief in the Thirty-Nine Articles after he had preached against them, and miracles, in the Cathedral. And canons are very difficult to convert, I am told."

"Then she is a good woman. And is Lord Reggie fond of her?"

"Oh yes, very. He spent a week with her last year, and I think he intends to spend another this year. She is very pleased about it. He and Mr. Amarinth are going down for the hop-picking."

"What a strange idea!"

"Yes, deliciously original. They say that hop-picking is quite Arcadian. Mr. Amarinth is having a little pipe made for him at Chappell's or somewhere, and he is going to sit under a tree and play old tunes by Scarlatti to the hop-pickers while they are at work. He says that more good can be done in that sort of way, than by all the missionaries who were ever eaten by savages. I don't believe much in missionaries."

"Do you believe in Mr. Amarinth?"

"Certainly. He is so witty. He gives one thoughts too, and that saves one such a lot of trouble. People who keep looking about in their own minds for thoughts are always so stupid. Mr. Amarinth gives you enough thoughts in an hour to last you for a couple of days."

"I doubt if they are worth very much. I suppose he gives Lord Reggie all his thoughts?"

"Yes, I dare say. He supplies half London, I believe. There is always some one of that kind going about. And as to his epigrams, they are in every one's mouth."

"That must make them rather monotonous," said Lady Locke, as the horses' heads were turned homewards, and they rolled smoothly towards Belgrave Square.

In the drawing-room they found a very thin, short-sighted-looking woman sitting quietly, apparently engaged in examining the picture and ornaments through a double eyeglass with a slender tortoise-shell stalk, which she held in her hand. She had a curious face, with a long, rather Jewish nose, and a thin-lipped mouth, a face wrinkled about the small eyes, above which was pasted a thick fringe of light brown hair covered with a visible "invisible" net.

"Madame Valtesi!" exclaimed Mrs. Windsor. "You have come in person to give me your answer about my week? That is charming. Are you coming out into the desert with us? Let me introduce my cousin, Lady Locke—Madame Valtesi."

The thin lady bowed peeringly. She seemed very blind indeed. Then she said, in a voice perhaps twenty years older than her middle-aged face, "How do you do? Yes, I will play the hermit with pleasure. I came to say so. You go down next Tuesday, or is it Wednesday?"

"On Wednesday. We shall be a charming little party, and so witty. Lord Reginald Hastings and Mr. Amarinth are both coming, and Mr. Tyler. My cousin and I complete the sextet. Oh! I had forgotten Tommy. But he does not count, not as a wit, I mean. He is my cousin's little boy. He is to play about with the curate's children. That will be so elevating for him."

"Delightful," said Madame Valtesi, with a face of stone. "No tea, thank you. I only stopped to tell you. I have three parties this afternoon. Good-bye. To-morrow morning I am going to get my trousseau for the desert, a shady garden hat, and gloves with gauntlets, and a walking-cane."

She gave a little croaking laugh with a cleverly taken girlish note at the end of it, and walked very slowly and quietly out of the room.

"I am so glad she can come," said Mrs. Windsor. "She makes our rustic party complete."

"We shall certainly be very rustic," said Lady Locke, with a smile, as she leaned back in her chair and took a cup of tea.

"Yes, deliciously so. Madame Valtesi goes everywhere. She is one of the most entertaining people in London. Nobody knows who she is. I have heard that she is a Russian spy, and that her husband was a courier, or a chef, or perhaps both. She has got some marvellous diamond earrings that were given to her by a Grand Duke, and she has lots of money. She runs a theatre, because she likes a certain actor, and she pays Mr. Amarinth's younger brother to go about with her and converse. He is very fat, and very uncouth, but he talks well. Madame Valtesi has a great deal of influence."

"In what department of life?"

"Oh—er—in every department, I believe. I really think my week will be a success this year. Last year. it was rather a failure. I took down Professor Smith, and he had a fit. So inconsiderate of him. In the country, too, where it is so difficult to get a doctor. We had in the veterinary surgeon in a hurry, but all he could say was 'Fire him!' and as I was not very intimate with the Professor, I hardly liked to do that. He has such a very violent temper. This year we shall have a good deal of music. Lord Reggie and Mr. Amarinth both play, and they are arranging a little programme. All old music, you know. They hate Wagner and the Moderns. They prefer the ancient church music, Mozart and Haydn and Paganini, or is it Palestrina? —I never can remember—and that sort of thing, so refining. Mr. Amarinth says that nothing has been done in music for the last hundred years. Personally, I prefer the Intermezzo out of 'Cavalleria' to anything I ever heard, but of course I am wrong. You have finished? Then I think I shall go and lie down before dressing for dinner. It is so hot. A breath of country air will be delicious."

"Yes, I confess I am looking forward with interest to the Surrey week," said Lady Locke, still smiling.

V

RS. WINDSOR'S cottage in Surrey stood on the outskirts of a perfectly charming village called Chenecote, a village just like those so often described in novels of the day. The homes of the poor people were model homes, with lattice windows, and modern improvements. The church was very small, but very trim. The windows were filled with stained glass, designed by Burne-Jones and executed by Morris, and there was a lovely little organ built by Willis, with a *vox humana* stop in it, that was like the most pathetic sheep that ever bleated to its lamb. The church and the red-tiled schoolhouse stood upon a delightful green common, covered with gorse bushes. There were trees all over the place, and the birds always sang in them. Roses bloomed in the neat little cottage gardens, and cheery, rosy children played happily about in the light sandy roads. Nothing, in fact, was wanting to make up a pretty picture of complete and English rusticity.

But Mrs. Windsor's cottage was the most charming picture of all. It was really a rambling thatched bungalow, with wide verandas trellised with dog roses, and a demure cosy garden full of velvet lawns and yew hedges cut into monstrous shapes. A tiny drive led up to the wide porch, and a neat green gate guarded the drive from the country road, beyond which there stood a regular George Morland village pond, a pond with muddy water, and fat geese, and ducks standing on their heads, and great sleek cart-horses pausing knee-deep to drink, with velvety distended nostrils, and, in fact, all the proper pond accessories. A little way up the road stood the curate's neat red house, and beyond that the village post-office and grocery store. Further away still were the substantial rectory, the model cottages, the common, the church, and schoolhouse. Behind the bungalow, which was called "The Retreat," there was a farmyard in which hens laid eggs for the bungalow breakfast table, and black Berkshire pigs slowly ripened and matured in the bright June sunshine. A stone sun-dial stood upon one of the velvet lawns, engraved with the legend "Tempus fugit," and various creaking basket and beehive chairs stood about, while no tennis net was permitted to desecrate the appearance of complete repose that the green garden presented to the tired town eye.

Mrs. Windsor declared that her guests must be content to rough it during the Surrey week; but as she took down with her from London a French chef and a couple of tall footmen, a carriage and pair, a governess cart, a fat white pony, a coachman and various housemaids, the guests regarded that dismal prospect with a fair amount of equanimity, and were assailed by none of those fears that appal the wanderer who arrives at a country inn or at a small lodging by the seaside. It may be pleasant to have roughed it, but it is always tiresome to be plunged in a frightful present instead of living gloriously upon a frightful past. If Mrs. Windsor's guests were deprived of the latter triumph, they at least were saved from the endurance of the former purgatory, and being for the most part entirely unheroic, they were not ill content. Rusticity in the rough they would decidedly not have approved of; rusticity in the smooth they liked very well. Mrs. Windsor was wise in her generation. She was distinctly not a clever woman, but she distinctly knew her world. The two tall footmen were the motto of her social life. She and Lady Locke, and the latter's little boy Tommy, came down from London by train in the morning of the Wednesday on which the Surrey week was to begin. The rest of the party were to assemble in the afternoon in time for tea. Tommy was in a state of almost painful excitement, as the train ran very slowly indeed through the pleasant country towards Dorking. He was a plump little boy, with rosy cheeks, big brown eyes, and a very round head, covered with exceedingly short brown hair. His age was nine, and he wore dark blue knickerbockers and a loose, bulgy sort of white shirt, trimmed with blue, and ornamented with a wide and flapping collar. His black stockings covered frisky legs, and his mind at present was mainly occupied with surmises as to the curate's little boys, with whom Mrs. Windsor had promised that he should play. He was a sharp child, interrogative in mind, and extremely loquacious. Mrs. Windsor found him rather trying. But then she was not accustomed to children, possessing, as she often boasted, none of her own.

"What are their names?" said Tommy, bounding suddenly from the window and squatting down before Mrs. Windsor, with his elbows on his blue serge knees, his firm white chin resting on his upturned palms, and his brown eyes fixed steadily upon her carefully arranged face, which always puzzled him very much; it was so unlike his mother's. "What are their names? Are any of them called Tommy?"

"I don't think so," she replied. "One of them is called Athanasius, I believe. I forget about the others."

"Why is he called Athanasius?"

"After the great Athanasius, I suppose."

"And who was the great Athanasius?"

"Oh—the well—well, he wrote a creed, Tommy; but you couldn't understand about that yet. You are too young."

"I don't think you know who the great Athanasius was much, Cousin Betty," said the boy, scrutinising her very closely, and trying to discover why her hair was so very light and her eyebrows were so very dark. "And you say they all wear spectacles. Can't they see without?"

Mrs. Windsor looked rather distractedly towards Lady Locke, who was reading a military article in the *Pall Mall Magazine* with deep attention.

"They can see a little without, I suppose, but not very much."

"Then are they blind?"

"No, only short-sighted. And then their father is a clergyman, you know, and clergymen generally wear spectacles. So perhaps they inherit it."

"What! the spectacles?"

"No, the—I mean they may require to wear spectacles because their father did before them. It is often so. But you are too young to understand heredity."

"I *can* understand things, Cousin Betty," said the boy rather severely.

"That's right. Well now, go and look out of the window. Look, there is a mill with the wheel turning, and a pond with a boat on it. What a dear little boat!"

Tommy went, obediently, but a little disdainfully, and Mrs. Windsor sank back in her seat feeling quite worn-out. She could cope better with the wits of a wit than with the wits of a child. She began to wish that Tommy was not going to make a part of the Surrey week. If he did not take a fancy to the curate's children after all, he would be thrown upon her hands. The prospect was rather terrible. However, she determined not to dwell upon it. It was no use to meet a possible trouble half-way. She closed her eyes, and wondered vaguely who the great Athanasius had really been till the train slowed down—it seemed to have been slowing down steadily all the way from Waterloo—and they drew up beside the platform at Dorking. Then Tommy was packed with his mother's maid into the governess cart with the fat white pony, which enchanted him to madness, and Lady Locke and Mrs. Windsor were driven away in the landau towards "The Retreat."

The day was radiantly fine, and very hot. The hedgerows were rather dusty, and the air was dim with a delicious haze that threw an atmosphere of enchantment round even the most commonplace objects. Dorking looked, as it always does, solid, serene, and cheerful, the beau-ideal of a prosperous country town, well-fed, well-groomed, well-favoured. Some of the shopkeepers were standing at their doors in their shirt-sleeves taking the air. The errand-boys whistled boisterously as they went about their business, and the butchers' carts dashed hither and thither with their usual spanking irresponsibility. Lady Locke looked about her with supreme contentment. She loved the English flavour of the place. It came upon her with all the charm of old-time recollections. Ten years had elapsed since she had strolled about an English village, or driven through an English country town. Her eyes suddenly filled with tears, and yet she was not unhappy. It was, on the contrary, the subtlety of her happiness that made her heart throb, and brought a choky feeling into her throat. Her tears were the idle ones, that are the sweetest tears of all.

Mrs. Windsor was not subtly happy. She never was. Sometimes she was irresponsibly cheerful, and generally she was lively, especially when there were any men about; but though she read much minor poetry, and knew all the minor poets, she was not poetic, and she honestly thought that John Gray's "Silver Points" were far finer literature than Wordsworth's "Ode to Immortality," or Rossetti's "Blessed Damosel." She liked sugar and water, especially when the sugar was very sweet, and the water very cloudy. As they drove through the High Street, she exclaimed—

"Look, Emily, there goes George Meredith into the post-office. How like he is to Watts's portrait of him! I never can get him to come near me, although I have read all his books. Mr. Amarinth says that he is going to bring out a new edition of them, 'done into English' by himself. It is such a good idea, and would help the readers so much. I believe he could make a lot of money by it, but it would be very difficult to do, I suppose. However, Mr. Amarinth is so clever that he might manage it. We shall soon be there now. Just look at Tommy! I do believe they are letting him drive."

Loud shouts of boyish triumph from in front in fact announced this divine consummation of happiness, and Tommy's face, wreathed in excited smiles, was turned round towards them, to attract their attention to his deeds of prowess. The fat white pony, evidently under the horrified impression that the son of Nimshi had suddenly mounted behind him, broke into a laborious and sprawling gallop, and, amid clouds of dust, the governess cart vanished down the hill, Lady Locke's maid striking attitudes of terror, and the smart groom shaking his slim and belted sides with laughter.

Lady Locke winked her tears away, and smiled.

"He is in the seventh heaven," she said.

"I only hope he won't be in the road directly," rejoined her cousin. "Ah! here is the village at last."

That afternoon, at four o'clock, a telegram arrived. It was from Mr. Tyler, and stated that he had caught the influenza, and could not come. Mrs. Windsor was much annoyed.

"Oh dear, I do hope my week is not going all wrong again this year!" she exclaimed plaintively. "I cannot fill his place now. Everybody is so full of engagements at this time of the year. We shall be a man short."

"Never mind, Betty," said her cousin. "Tommy is quite a man in his own eyes, and I rather like being a little neglected sometimes. It is restful."

"Do you think so? Well, perhaps you are right. Men are not always soothing. Let us go out into the garden. The others ought to be here directly, unless they have got the influenza too. I am thankful Mr. Tyler did not have it here. It would be worse than a fit. A fit only lasts for a few minutes after all, and then it is not catching, which is such a consolation. Really, when one comes to think of it, a fit is one of the best things one can have, if one is to have anything. We are going to take tea here under the cedar tree."

Lady Locke opened her well-formed rather ample mouth, and drew in a deep breath of country air. She had no sort of feeling about the absence of Mr. Tyler, whom she had never seen. The country, and the warmth, and the summer were quite enough for her. Still, she looked forward to studying Lord Reggie with an eagerness that she hardly acknowledged even to herself. She hoped vaguely that he would be different in the country, that he would put on a country mind with his country clothes, that his brain would work more naturally under a straw hat, and that in canvas shoes he might find a certain amount of salvation. At any rate, he would look delightfully cool and young on the velvet lawn under the great cedar. That was certain. And his whimsicalities were generally amusing, and sometimes original. As to Mr. Amarinth, she could not imagine him in the country at all. He smacked essentially of cities. What he would do in this *galère* she knew not. She leaned back in her basket-chair and enjoyed herself quietly. The green peace, after London, was absolutely delicious. She could hear a hen clucking intermittently from the farmyard hard by, the twitter of birds from the yew-trees, the chirping voices of Tommy and the curate's little boys, who had been formally introduced to each other, and had retired to play in a paddock that was part of the rector's glebe. The rector himself was away on a holiday, and the curate was doing all the work for the time. Big golden bees buzzed slowly and pertinaciously in and out of the sweet flowers in the formal rose garden, chaunting a note that was like the diapason of some distant organ. Mrs. Windsor's pug, "Bung," lay on his fat side in the sun with half-closed eyes, snoring loudly to indicate the fact that he seriously meditated dropping into a doze. All the air was full of mingled magical scents, hanging on the tiny breeze that stole softly about among the leaves and flowers. There was a clink of china and silver in the cottage, for the tall footmen were preparing to bring out the tea. How pleasant it all was! Lady Locke felt half inclined to snore with her eyes open, like Bung. It seemed such a singularly appropriate tribute to the influence of place and weather. However she restrained herself, and merely folded her hands in her lap and fell into a waking dream.

She was roused by the scrunch of carriage wheels on the gravel drive.

"There they are!" said Mrs. Windsor, springing from her chair with vivacious alacrity. "The train has been punctual for once in its life. How shocked the directors would be if they knew it, but, of course, it will be kept from them. Ah! Madame Valtesi, so glad to see you! How do, Lord Reggie? How do, Mr. Amarinth? So you all came together! This is such a mercy, as I have only one carriage down here except the cart, which doesn't count. I told you we should have to rough it, didn't I? That is part of the attraction of the week. Simplicity in all things, you know, especially carriages. Mr. Tyler

can't come. Isn't it shocking? Influenza. London is so full of microbes. Do microbes go to parties, Mr. Amarinth? because Mr.
Tyler lives entirely at parties. He must have caught it in Society.
Will you have tea before you go to your rooms? Yes, do. Here it
comes. We are going to have country strawberries and penny buns
made in the village, and quite hot! So rustic and wholesome! After
all, it is nice to eat something wholesome just once in a while, isn't
it?"

Her guests settled into the arm-chairs, and Bung, who had risen
in some pardonable fury, lay down again and prepared to resume
his interrupted meditations.

Madame Valtesi was already attired in her trousseau. She had
travelled down from London in a shady straw hat trimmed with
pink roses. A white veil swept loosely round her face; she carried in
her hand an attenuated mottled cane, with an elaborate silver top.
A black fan hung from her waist by a thin silver chain, and, as usual,
she was peering through her eyeglasses at her surroundings. Mr.
Amarinth and Lord Reggie were dressed very much alike in loosely
fitting very light suits, with high turn-down collars, all-round collars
that somehow suggested babyhood and innocence, and loosely
knotted ties. They wore straw hats, suède gloves, and brown boots,
and in their buttonholes large green carnations bloomed savagely.
They looked very cool, very much at their ease, and very well
inclined for tea. Reggie's face was rather white, and the look in his
blue eyes suggested that London was getting altogether the better
of him.

"Wholesome things almost always disagree with me," said
Madame Valtesi, in her croaky voice, "unless I eat them at the
wrong time. Now, a hot bun before breakfast in the morning, or in
bed at night, might suit me admirably; but if I ate one now, I should
feel miserable. Your strawberries look most original, quite the real
thing. Do not be angry with me for discarding the buns. If I ate one,
I should really infallibly lose my temper."

"How curious," said Mr. Amarinth, taking a bun delicately between his plump white fingers. "My temper and my heart are the
only two things I never lose! Everything else vanishes. I think the art
of losing things is a very subtle art. So few people can lose anything
really beautifully. Anybody can find a thing. That is so simple. A
crossing sweeper can discover a sixpence lying in the road. It is the
crossing sweeper who loses a sixpence who shows real originality."

"I wish I could find a few sixpences," said Madame Valtesi slowly, and sipping her tea with her usual air of stony gravity. "Times are so very bad. Do you know, Mr. Amarinth, I am almost afraid I shall have to put down my carriage, or your brother. I cannot keep them both up, and pay my dressmaker's bill too. I told him so yesterday. He was very much cut up."

"Poor Teddy! Have his conversational powers gone off? I never see him. The world is so very large, isn't it?"

"No, he still talks rather well." Then she added, turning to Lady Locke, "You know I always give him five shillings an hour, in generous moments ten, to take me about and talk to me. He is a superb *raconteur*. I shall miss him very much."

"The profession of a conversationalist is so delightful," said Mrs. Windsor, "I wonder more people don't follow it. You are too generous, Esmé; you took it up out of pure love of the thing."

"The true artist will always be an amateur," said Lord Reggie dreamily, and gazing towards Lady Locke with abstracted blue eyes, "just as the true martyr will always live for his faith. Esmé is like the thrush. He always tells us his epigrams twice over, lest we should fail to capture their first fine careful rapture. Repetition is one of the secrets of success nowadays. Esmé was the first conversationalist in England to discover that fact, and so he won his present unrivalled position, and has known how to keep it."

"Conversational powers are sometimes very distressing," said Madame Valtesi. "Last winter I was having my house in Cromwell Road painted and papered. I went to live at a hotel, but the men were so slow, that at last I took possession again, hoping to turn them out. It was a most fatal step. They liked me so much, and found me so entertaining, that they have never gone away. They are still painting, and I suppose always will be. Whenever I say anything witty they scream with laughter, and I believe that my name has become a household word in Whitechapel or Wapping, or wherever the British workman lives. What am I to do?"

"Read them Jerome K. Jerome's last comic book," said Amarinth, "and they will go at once. I find his works most useful. I always begin to quote from them when I wish to rid myself of a bore."

"But surely he is a very entertaining writer," said Lady Locke.

"My dear lady, if you read him you will find that he is the reverse of Beerbohm Tree as Hamlet. Tree's Hamlet was funny without being vulgar. Jerome's writings are vulgar without being funny. His books are like Academy pictures. They are all deserving of a place on the line."

"I think he means well," said Mrs. Windsor, taking some strawberries.

"I am afraid so," Amarinth answered. "People who mean well always do badly. They are like the ladies who wear clothes that don't fit them in order to show their piety. Good intentions are invariably ungrammatical."

"Good intentions have been the ruin of the world," said Reggie fervently. "The only people who have achieved anything have been those who have had no intentions at all. I have no intentions."

"You will at least never be involved in an action for breach of promise if you always state that fact," said Lady Locke, laughing.

"To be intentional is to be middle class," remarked Amarinth. "Herkomer has become intentional, and so he has taken to painting the directors of railway companies. The great picture of this year's exhibition is intentional. The great picture of the year always is. It presents to us a pretty milkmaid milking her cow. A gallant, riding by, has dismounted, and is kissing the milkmaid."

Madame Valtesi blinked at him for a moment in silence. Then she said, with an air of indescribable virtue—

"What a bad example for the cow!"

"Ah! I never thought of that!" cried Mrs. Windsor.

"One seldom does think how easily proper cows—and people— are put to confusion. That is why they so often flee the plays of London to those of Paris. They can be confused there without their relations knowing it."

"Why are old men who have seen the world always so proper?" asked Lord Reggie. "The other day I was staying with an old general at Malta, and he took Catulle Mendez' charming and delicate romance, 'Mephistophela,' out of my bedroom and burnt it. Yet his language on parade was really quite artistically blasphemous. I think it is fatal to one's personality to see the world at all."

"Then I must be quite hopeless," said Lady Locke, "for I have spent eight years in the Straits Settlements."

"Dear me!" murmured Madame Valtesi. "Where is that? It sounds like one of the places where that geographical little Henry Arthur Jones sends the heroes of his plays to expiate their virtues."

"It is quite a mistake to imagine that the author or the artist should stuff his beautiful, empty mind with knowledge, with impressions, with facts of any kind," said Amarinth. "I have written a great novel upon Iceland, full of colour, of passion, of the most subtle impurity, yet I could not point you out Iceland upon the map. I do not know where it is, or what it is. I only know that it has a beautiful name, and that I have written a beautiful thing about it. This age is an age of identification, in which our god is the Encyclopædia Britannica, and our devil the fairy tale that teaches nothing. We go to the British Museum for culture, and to Archdeacon Farrar for guidance. And then we think that we are advancing. We might as well return to the myths of Darwin, or to the delicious fantasies of John Stuart Mill. They at least were entertaining, and no one attempted to believe in them."

"We always return to our first hates," said Lord Reggie, rather languidly.

"Do have some more tea, Madame Valtesi," pleaded Mrs. Windsor.

"No, thank you. I never take more than one cup on principle—the principle being that the first cup is the best, like the last word. I want to take a stroll round the rose garden, if I may. Mr. Amarinth, will you come with me?"

She added in an undertone to him, as they walked slowly away together—

"I always hate to see people drinking when I have finished. It makes me feel like a barmaid."

VI

ADY LOCKE and Lord Reggie were left alone together for the time. Mrs. Windsor had gone into the cottage to write a note, asking the curate of Chenecote to dine the next day. She always asked the curate to dine during the Surrey week. She thought it made things so deliciously rustic. Lord Reggie was still looking very tired, and eating a great many strawberries. He did both mechanically, and as if he didn't know he was doing them. As Lady Locke glanced at him, she felt that he certainly fulfilled her expectations, so far as being cool and young went. His round baby collar seemed to take off quite five years from his age, and his straw hat, with its black riband, suited him very well. Only the glaring green carnation offended her sight. She longed to ask him why he wore it. But she felt she had no right to. So she watched him looking tired and eating strawberries, until he glanced up at her with his pretty blue eyes.

"These strawberries are very good," he said. "I should finish them, only I hate finishing anything. There is something so commonplace about it. Don't you think so? Commonplace people are always finishing off things, and getting through things. They map out their days, and have special hours for everything. I should like to have special hours for nothing. That would be much more original."

"You are very fond of originality?"

"Are not you?"

"I don't quite know. Perhaps I have not met many original people in my life. You see I have been out of England a great deal, and out of cities. I have lived almost entirely among soldiers."

"Soldiers are never original. They think it is unmanly. I once spent a week with the commander of one of our armies of occupation, and I never heard the same remarks so often in all my life. They thought everything was an affectation. Once, when I mentioned Matthew Arnold at the mess, they thought he was an affectation."

"Oh, surely not."

"They did, really. I explained that he had been a school-inspector.

I thought that might reassure them. But they evidently did not believe me. They knew nothing about anything or anybody. That would have been rather charming, only they thought they knew everything."

"I think you must have been unfortunate in your experience."

"Perhaps I was. I know I tried to be manly. I talked about Wilson Barrett. What more could I do? To talk about Wilson Barrett is generally supposed to show your appreciation of the heroic age. Of course nobody thinks about him now. But I was quite a failure. I went to five dinner-parties, I remember, during that week, and we all conversed about machine-guns at each of them. I felt as if the whole of life was a machine-gun, and men and women were all quick-firing parties."

"I suppose we are most of us a little inclined to talk shop, as it is called."

"But we ought to talk general shop, the shop in which everything is sold from Bibles to cheap cheese. Only we might leave out the Bibles. Mrs. Humphry Ward has created a corner in them."

"You have finished the strawberries after all."

Reggie burst into an almost boyish laugh.

"So I have. We none of us live up to our ideals, I suppose. But really I have none. I agree with Esmé that nothing is so limited as to have an ideal."

"And yet you look sometimes as if you might have many," she said, as if half to herself. The curious motherly feeling had come upon her again, a kind of tenderness that often leads to preaching.

Reggie glanced up at her quickly, and with a pleased expression. A veiled tribute to his good looks delighted him, whether it came from man or woman. Only an unveiled one surpassed it in his estimation.

"Ah! but that means nothing," he said. "It is quite a mistake to believe, as many people do, that the mind shows itself in the face. Vice may sometimes write itself in lines and changes of contour, but that is all. Our faces are really masks given to us to conceal our minds with. Of course occasionally the mask slips partly off, generally when we are stupid and emotional. But that is an inartistic accident. Outward revelations of what is going on inside of us take place far more seldom than silly people suppose. No more preposterous theory has ever been put forward than that of the artist revealing himself in his art. The writer, for instance, has at least

three minds—his Society mind, his writing mind, and his real mind.
They are all quite separate and distinct, or they ought to be. When
his writing mind and his real mind get mixed up together, he ceases
to be an artist. That is why Swinburne has gone off so much. If you
want to write really fine erotic poetry, you must live an absolutely
rigid and entirely respectable life. The 'Laus Veneris' could only
have been produced by a man who had a Nonconformist conscience.
I am certain that Mrs. Humphry Ward is the most strictly orthodox
Christian whom we have. Otherwise, her books against the accepted
Christianity could never have brought her in so many thousands of
pounds. I never read her, of course. Life is far too long and lovely for
that sort of thing; but a bishop once told me that she was a great
artist, and that if she had a sense of gravity, she would rival George
Eliot. Dickens had probably no sense of humour. That is why he
makes second-rate people die of laughing. Oscar Wilde was utterly
mistaken when he wrote the 'Picture of Dorian Gray.' After Dorian's
act of cruelty, the picture ought to have grown more sweet, more
saintly, more angelic in expression."

"I never read that book."

"Then you have gained a great deal. Poor Oscar! He is terribly
truthful. He reminds me so much of George Washington."

"Shall we walk round the garden if you have really finished tea?"
said Lady Locke, rising. "What a delicious afternoon it is, so quiet, so
detached from the rest of the year, as Mr. Amarinth might say.
I am glad to be away from London. It is only habit that makes London endurable."

"But surely habit makes nothing endurable. Otherwise we should
like politics, and get accustomed to the presence of solicitors in
Society."

"I do like politics," Lady Locke said, laughing. "How beautiful
these roses are! Ah, there is Tommy. You don't know my little boy,
do you?" Tommy, in fact, now came bounding towards them
along a rose alley. His cheeks were flushed with excitement, and, as
he drew nearer, they saw that his brown eyes were sparkling with a
dimmed lustre behind a large pair of spectacles, that were set
rakishly upon his straight little nose.

"My dear boy," exclaimed his mother, "what on earth are you
doing? How hideous you are!"

"Harry Smith has lent them to me," cried Tommy exultantly.
"He says I look splendid in them."

"That is all very fine, but Harry Smith requires them, and you don't. His father won't like it. You must give them back, Tommy. Shake hands with Lord Reginald Hastings. He has come to stay here."

Tommy shook hands scrutinisingly, and at once broke conversational ground with—

"Do you know who the great Athanasius was?"

"He was an excellent person, who will always be widely known to fame for his omissions. He did not write the Athanasian Creed. For that reason he will always be deserving of our respect."

Tommy listened to these remarks with profound attention, and expressed himself very well satisfied with this addition to his youthful knowledge. He thrust his hot hand into Lord Reggie's with the artless remark—

"You are more clever than Cousin Betty!" and invited him to join forthwith in a game of ball upon the bowling-green. To Lady Locke's surprise, Lord Reggie did not resist the alluring temptation, but ran off with the boy quite light-heartedly. She stood watching them as they disappeared across the smooth green lawn.

"I can't understand him," she thought to herself. "He seems to be talented, and yet an echo of another man, naturally good-hearted, full of horrible absurdities, a gentleman, and yet not a man at all. He says himself that he commits every sin that attracts him, but he does not look wicked. What is he? Is he being himself, or is he being Mr. Amarinth, or is he merely posing, or is he really hateful, or is he only whimsical, and clever, and absurd? What would he have been if he had never seen Mr. Amarinth?"

She began vaguely to dislike Mr. Amarinth, vaguely to like Lord Reggie. Her boy had taken a fancy to him, and she was an unreasonably motherly mother. People who are unreasonably motherly like by impulse wholly very often, and hate by impulse. Their mind has no why or wherefore with which to bolster up their heart. She went slowly towards the cottage to dress for dinner, and all the time that she was walking, she continued, rather strenuously, to like Lord Reggie.

That evening, after dinner, there was music in the small drawing-room, which was exquisitely done up in Eastern style, with an arched roof, screens of wonderfully carved wood brought from Upper Egypt, Persian hangings and embroideries, divans and prayer rugs, on which nobody ever prayed. Lord Reggie and Mr. Amarinth both played the piano in an easy, tentative sort of way, making excess of expression do duty for deficiencies of execution, and covering occasional mistakes with the soft rather than with the loud pedal. Lord Reggie played a hymn of his own, which he frankly acknowledged was very beautiful. He described it as a hymn without words, which, he said softly, all hymns should be. There was archaic simplicity, not to say baldness, about it which sent Mrs. Windsor into exotic raptures, and, as it was exceedingly short, it made its definite mark.

There was a moon in the night, full, round, and serene, and the French windows stood open to the quiet garden. The drawing-room was very dimly lighted, and as Reggie played, he was in shadow. His white, sensitive face was only faintly to be seen. It looked pure and young, Lady Locke thought, as she watched him. He was so enamoured of his hymn that he played it over and over again, and, from his touch, it seemed as if he were trying to make the Steinway grand sound as much like a spinet as possible.

Madame Valtesi sat on a sofa with her long, slim feet supported upon an embroidered cushion. She was smoking a cigarette with all the complete mastery of custom. Mrs. Windsor stood near the window, idly following with her eyes the perambulations of Bung, who was flitting about the garden like a ghost with a curled tail and a turned-up nose. Mr. Amarinth leaned largely upon the piano, in an attitude of rapt attention. His clever, clean-shaved face wore an expression of seraphic sensuality.

Lady Locke listened quietly. She had never heard any hymn so often before, and yet she did not feel bored.

At last Lord Reggie stopped, and said, "Esmé, the curate comes to dine to-morrow. Remember to be very sweet to him. I want to play the organ on Sunday morning, and he must let us do an anthem. I will compose one. We can get up a choir practice on Friday night, if Mrs. Windsor does not mind."

"Oh, charming!" Mrs. Windsor cried from the window. "I love a choir practice above all things. Choir boys are so pretty. They must come to the practice in their night-gowns, of course. I am sure Mr. Smith will be delighted. But you must remember to be very High Church to-morrow night. Mr. Smith is terribly particular about that."

"I don't think I know how to be High Church," said Madame Valtesi very gravely. "Does one assume any special posture of body, or are one's convictions to be shown only in attitude of mind?"

"Oh, there is no difficulty," said Lord Reggie. "All one has to do is to abuse the Evangelical party. Speak disrespectfully of the Bishop of Liverpool, and say that Father Staunton and the Bishop of Lincoln are the only preachers of true doctrine in England. The Ritualists are very easily pleased. They put their faith in preachers and in postures. If I were anything, I would be a Roman Catholic."

"Should you like to confess all your sins?" asked Lady Locke, in some surprise.

"Immensely. There is nothing so interesting as telling a good man or woman how bad one has been. It is intellectually fascinating. One of the greatest pleasures of having been what is called wicked is, that one has so much to say to the good. Good people love hearing about sin. Haven't you noticed that although the sinner takes no sort of interest in the saint, the saint has always an uneasy curiosity about the doings of the sinner? It is a case of the County Council and Zaeo's back over and over again."

"Yes, we love examining each other's backs," said Madame Valtesi.

Esmé Amarinth sighed musically and very loudly, and remarked—

"Faith is the most plural thing I know. We are all supposed to believe in the same thing in different ways. It is like eating out of the same dish with different coloured spoons. And we beat each other with the spoons, like children."

"And the dish gives us indigestion," said Madame Valtesi. "I once spent a week with an aunt who had taken to Litany, as other people take to dram-drinking, you know. We went to Litany every day, and I never had so much dyspepsia before in my life. Litany, taken often, is more indigestible than lobster at midnight."

"How exquisite the moon is!" said Lady Locke, rising and going towards the window.

"The moon is the religion of the night," said Esmé. "Go out into the garden all of you, and I will sing you a song of the moon. It is very beautiful. I shall give it to Jean de Reszke, I think. My voice will sound better from a distance. Good voices always do."

He sat down at the piano, and they strolled out through the French windows into the green and silent pleasaunce.

His voice was clear and open, and he spoke rather than sang the following verses, while they stood listening till the rippling accompaniment trickled away into silence:—

"Oh! beautiful moon with the ghostly face,
   Oh! moon with the brows of snow,
Rise up, rise up from your slumbering place,
   And draw from your eyes the veil,
Lest my wayward heart should fail
   In the homage it fain would bestow—
Oh! beautiful moon with the ghostly face,
   Oh! moon with the brows of snow.

Oh! beautiful mouth like a scarlet flow'r,
   Oh! mouth with the wild, soft breath,
Kiss close, kiss close in the dream-stricken bow'r,
   And whisper away the world;
Till the wayward wings are furled,
   And the shadow is lifted from death—
Oh! beautiful mouth like a scarlet flow'r,
   Oh! mouth with the wild, soft breath!

Oh! beautiful soul with the outstretched hands,
   Oh! soul with the yearning eyes,
Lie still, lie still in the fairy lands
   Where never a tear may fall;
Where no voices ever call
   Any passion-act, strange or unwise—
Oh! beautiful soul with the outstretched hands,
   Oh! soul with the yearning eyes!"

The song was uttered with so much apparent passion, that Lady Locke felt tears standing in her eyes when the last word ceased on the cool air of the night.

"How beautiful," she said involuntarily to Lord Reggie, who happened to be standing beside her. "And how wrong!"

"Surely that is a contradiction in terms," the boy said. "Nothing that is beautiful can possibly be wrong."

"Then how exquisitely right some women have been whom Society has hounded out of its good graces," Madame Valtesi remarked.

"Yes," said Reggie. "And how exquisitely happy in their rectitude."

"But not in their punishment," said Mrs. Windsor. "I think it is so silly to give people the chance of whipping you for what they do themselves."

"Society only loves one thing more than sinning," said Madame Valtesi, examining the moon magisterially through her tortoiseshell eyeglass.

"And what is that?" said Lady Locke.

"Administering injustice."

VII

ELL, what would you all like to do with yourselves to-day?" asked Mrs. Windsor on the following morning after breakfast, which was over at
half-past ten, for they all got up early as a mark
of respect to the country air; and indeed, Mr.
Amarinth declared that he had been awake before
five, revelling in the flame-coloured music of the farmyard cocks.

"I should like to go out shopping," remarked Madame Valtesi,
who was dressed in a white serge dress, figured with innocent pink
flowers.

"But, my dear, there are no shops!"

"There is always a linen-draper's in every village," said Madame
Valtesi; "and a grocer's."

"But what would you buy there?"

"That is just what I wish to know. May I have the governess cart?
I want to try and feel like a governess."

"Of course. I will order it. Will you drive yourself?"

"Oh no, I am too blind. Lady Locke, won't you come with me?
I am sure you can drive. I can always tell by looking at people what
they can do. I could pick you out a dentist from a crowd of a hundred
people."

"Or a driver?" said Lady Locke. "I think I can manage the white
pony. Yes, I will come with pleasure."

"I shall go into the drawing-room and compose my anthem for
Sunday," said Lord Reggie. "I am unlike Saint Saëns. I always
compose at the piano."

"And I will go into the rose-garden," said Esmé, "and eat pink
roses. There is nothing more delicious than a ripe La France. May I,
Mrs. Windsor? Please don't say 'This is Liberty Hall,' or I shall
think of Mr. Alexander, the good young manager who never dies—
but may I?"

"Do. And compose some Ritualistic epigrams to say to Mr. Smith
to-night. How delightfully rustic we all are! So naïve! I am going to
order dinner, and add up the household accounts for yesterday."

She rustled away with weary grace, rattling delicately a large bunch of keys that didn't open anything in particular. They were a part of her get up as a country hostess.

A few moments later some simple chords, and the sound of a rather obvious sequence, followed by intensely Handelian runs, announced that Lord Reggie had begun to compose his anthem, and Madame Valtesi and Lady Locke were mounting into the governess cart, which was rather like a large hip bath on wheels. They sat opposite to each other upon two low seats, and Lady Locke drove sideways.

As they jogged along down the dusty country road, between the sweet-smelling flowery banks, Madame Valtesi said—

"Do governesses always drive in tubs? Is it part of the system?"

"I don't know," answered Lady Locke, looking at the hunched white figure facing her, and at the little shrewd eyes peering from beneath the shade of the big and aggressive garden hat. "What system do you mean?"

"The English governess system; simple clothes, no friends, no society, no money, no late dinner, supper at nine, all the talents, and bed at ten whether you are inclined to sleep or not. Do they invariably go about in tubs as well?"

"I suppose very often. These carts are always called governess carts."

Madame Valtesi nodded enigmatically.

"I am glad I have never had to be a governess," said Lady Locke thoughtfully. "From a worldly point of view, I suppose I have been born under a lucky star."

"There is no such thing as luck in the world," Madame Valtesi remarked, putting up a huge white parasol that abruptly extinguished the view for miles. "There is only capability."

"But some capable people are surely unlucky."

"They are incapable in one direction or another. Have you not noticed that whenever a man is a failure his friends say he is an able man? No man is able who is unable to get on, just as no woman is clever who can't succeed in obtaining that worst, and most necessary, of evils—a husband."

"You are very cynical," said Lady Locke, flicking the pony's fat white back with the whip.

"All intelligent people are. Cynicism is merely the art of seeing things as they are instead of as they ought to be. If one says that Christianity has never converted the Christians, or that love has ruined more women than hate, or that virtue is an accident of environment, one is sure to be dubbed a cynic. And yet all these remarks are true to absolute absurdity."

"I scarcely think so."

"But then you have been in the Straits Settlements for eight years. They are true in London. And there are practically not more than about five universal truths in the world. One must always locate a truth if one wishes to be understood. What is true in London is often a lie in the country. I believe that there are still many good Christians in the country, but they are only good Christians because they are in the country—most of them. Our virtues are generally a fortunate, or unfortunate, accident, and the same may be said of our vices. Now, think of Lord Reggie. He is one of the most utterly vicious young men of the day. Why? Because, like the chameleon, he takes his colour from whatever he rests upon, or is put near. And he has been put near scarlet instead of white."

Lady Locke felt a strange thrill of pain at her heart.

"I am sure Lord Reggie has a great deal of good in him!" she exclaimed.

"Not enough to spoil his charm," said Madame Valtesi. "He has no real intention of being either bad or good. He lives like Esmé Amarinth, merely to be artistic."

"But what in Heaven's name does that word mean?" asked Lady Locke. "It seems almost the only modern word. I hear it everywhere like a sort of refrain."

"I cannot tell you. I am too old. Ask Lord Reggie. He would tell you anything."

The last words were spoken with slow intention.

"What do you mean?" said Lady Locke hastily.

"Here we are at the post-office. Would it not be the proper thing to do to get some stamps? No? Then let us stop at the linen-draper's. I feel a strong desire to buy some village frilling. And there are some deliciously coarse-looking pocket-handkerchiefs in the window, about a yard square. I must get a dozen of those."

At lunch that day Lord Reggie announced that he had composed a beautiful anthem on the words—

"Thy lips are like a thread of scarlet, and thy speech is comely; thy temples are like a piece of pomegranate within thy locks."

"They sound exactly like something of Esmé's," he said, "but really they are taken from the 'Song of Solomon.' I had no idea that the Bible was so intensely artistic. There are passages in the Book of Job that I should not be ashamed to have written."

"You remind me of a certain lady writer who is very popular in kitchen circles," said Esmé, "and whose husband once told me that she had founded her style upon Mr. Ruskin and the better parts of the Bible. She brings out about seven books every year, I am told, and they are all about sailors, of whom she knows absolutely nothing. I am perpetually meeting her, and she always asks me to lunch, and says she knows my brother. She seems to connect my poor brother with lunch in some curious way. I shall never lunch with her, but she will always ask me."

"Hope springs eternal in the human breast," Mrs. Windsor said, with a little air of aptness.

"That is one of the greatest fallacies of a melancholy age," Esmé answered, arranging the huge moonstone in his tie with a plump hand; "suicide would be the better word. 'The Second Mrs. Tanqueray' has made suicide quite the rage. A number of most respectable ladies, without the vestige of a past among them, have put an end to themselves lately, I am told. To die naturally has become most unfashionable, but no doubt the tide will turn presently."

"I wonder if people realise how dangerous they may be in their writings," said Lady Locke.

"One has to choose between being dangerous and being dull. Society loves to feel itself upon the edge of a precipice, I assure you. To be harmless is the most deadly enemy to social salvation. Strict respectability would even handicap a rich American nowadays, and rich Americans are terribly respectable by nature. That is why they are always so anxious to get into the Prince of Wales's set."

"I suppose Ibsen is responsible for a good deal," Mrs. Windsor said, rather vaguely. Luncheon always rendered her rather vague, and after food her intellect struggled for egress, as the sun struggles to emerge from behind intercepting clouds.

"I believe Mr. Clement Scott thinks so," said Amarinth; "but then it does not matter very much what Mr. Clement Scott thinks, does it? The position of the critics always strikes me as very comic. They are for ever running at the back of public opinion, and shouting 'Come on!' or 'Go back!' to those who are in front of them. If half of them had their way, our young actors and actresses would play in Pinero's pieces as Mrs. Siddons or Charles Kean played in the pieces of Shakespeare long ago. A good many of them found their claims to attention on the horrible fact that they once knew Charles Dickens, a circumstance of which they ought rather to be ashamed. They are monotonous dwellers in an unenlightened past like Mr. Sala, who is even more commonplace than the books of which he is for ever talking. Mr. Joseph Knight is their oracle at first nights, and some of them even labour under the wild impression that Mr. Robert Buchanan can write good English, and that Mr. George R. Sims—what would he be without the initial?—is a minor poet."

"Dear me! I am afraid we are all wrong," said Mrs. Windsor, still rather vaguely; "but do you know, we ought really to be thinking of our walk up Leith Hill. It is a lovely afternoon. Will you attempt it, Madame Valtesi?"

"No, thank you. I think I must have been constructed, like Providence, with a view to sitting down. Whoever thinks of the Deity as standing? I will stay at home and read the last number of 'The Yellow Disaster.' I want to see Mr. Aubrey Beardsley's idea of the Archbishop of Canterbury. He has drawn him sitting in a wheelbarrow in the gardens of Lambeth Palace, with underneath him the motto, 'J'y suis, j'y reste.' I believe he has on a black mask. Perhaps that is to conceal the likeness."

"I have seen it," Mrs. Windsor said; "it is very clever. There are only three lines in the whole picture, two for the wheelbarrow and one for the Archbishop."

"What exquisite simplicity!" said Lord Reggie, going out into the hall to get his straw hat.

In the evening, when they assembled in the drawing-room for dinner, it was found that both Mrs. Windsor and Madame Valtesi had put on simple black dresses in honour of the curate. Lady Locke, although she never wore widow's weeds, had given up colours since her husband's death. As they waited for Mr. Smith's advent there was an air of decent expectation about the party. Mr. Amarinth looked serious to heaviness. Lord Reggie was pale, and seemed abstracted. Probably he was thinking of his anthem, whose tonic and dominant chords, and diatonic progressions, he considered most subtly artistic. He would like to have written in the Lydian mode, only he could not remember what the Lydian mode was, and he had forgotten to bring any harmony book with him. He glanced into the mirror over the fireplace, smoothed his pale gold hair with his hand, and prepared to be very sweet to the curate in order to obtain possession of the organ on the ensuing Sunday.

"Mr. Smith," said one of the tall footmen, throwing open the drawing-room, and a tall, thin, ascetic-looking man, with a shaved dark face, and an incipient tonsure, entered the room very seriously.

"Dinner is served."

The two announcements followed one upon the other almost without pause. Mrs. Windsor requested the curate to take her in, after introducing him to her guests in the usual rather muddled and perfunctory manner. When they were all seated, and Mr. Amarinth was beginning to hold forth over the clear soup, she murmured confidentially to her companion—

"So good of you to take pity upon us. You will not find us very gay. We are really down here to have a quiet, serious week—a sort of retreat, you know. Mr. Amarinth is holding it. I hope nobody will have a fit this time. Ah! of course you did not come last year. Do you like Chenecote? A sweet village, isn't it?"

"Very sweet indeed, outwardly. But I fear there is a good deal to be done inwardly; much sweeping and scouring of minds before the savour of the place will be quite acceptable on high."

"Dear me! I am sorry to hear that. One can never tell, of course."

"I have put a stop to a good deal already, I am thankful to say. I have broken up the idle corners permanently, and checked the Sunday evening rowdyism upon the common."

"Indeed! I am so glad. Mr. Smith has broken up the idle corners, Madame Valtesi. Is it not a mercy?"

Madame Valtesi looked enigmatical, as indeed she always did when she was ignorant. She had not the smallest idea what an idle corner might be, nor how it could be broken up. She therefore peered through her eyeglasses and said nothing. Mr. Amarinth was less discreet.

"An idle corner," he said. "What a delicious name. It might have been invented by Izaak Walton. It suggests a picture by George Morland. I love his canvases, rustics carousing—"

But before he could get any further, Reggie caught his eye and formed silently with his lips the words, "Remember my anthem."

"He idealises so much," Amarinth went on easily. "Of course a real carouse is horribly inartistic. Excess always is, although Oscar Wilde has said that nothing succeeds like it."

"Excess is very evil," Mr. Smith said, rather rigidly. "Excess in everything seems to be characteristic of our age. I could wish that many would return to the ascetic life. No wine, thank you."

"Indeed, yes," said Mrs. Windsor, "that is what I always think. There is something so beautiful in not eating and drinking, and not marrying, and all that; but at least we must acknowledge that celibacy is quite coming into fashion. Our young men altogether refuse to marry nowadays. Let us hope that is a step in the right direction."

"If they married more and drank less, I don't fancy their morals would suffer much," Madame Valtesi remarked with exceeding dryness, looking at Mr. Smith's budding tonsure through her tortoise-shell eyeglass.

"The monastic life is very beautiful," said Lord Reggie. "I always find, when I go to a monastery, that the monks give me very excellent wine. I suppose they keep all their hair shirts for their own private use."

"That is the truest hospitality, isn't it?" said Lady Locke.

"The High Church party are showing us the right way," Mr. Amarinth remarked impressively, with a side anthem-glance at Lord Reggie which spoke volumes. "They understand the value of æstheticism in religion. They recognise the fact that a beautiful vestment uplifts the soul far more than a dozen bad chants by Stainer, or Barnby, or any other unmusical Christian. The average Anglican chant is one of the most unimaginative, unpoetical things in the world. It always reminds me of the cart-horse parade on Whit Monday. A brown Gregorian is so much more devotional."

"I beg your pardon," said Mr. Smith, who had been listening to these remarks with acquiescence, but who now manifested some obvious confusion.

"A brown Gregorian," Mr. Amarinth repeated. "All combinations of sounds convey a sense of colour to the mind. Gregorians are obviously of a rich and sombre brown, just as a Salvation Army hymn is a violent magenta."

"I think the Bishops are beginning to understand Gregorian music a little better. No plovers' eggs, thank you," said Mr. Smith, who was totally without a sense of melody, but who assumed a complete musical authority, based on the fact that he intoned in church.

"The Bishops never go on understanding anything," said Mr. Amarinth. "They conceal their intelligence, if they have any, up their lawn sleeves. I once met a bishop. It was at a garden party at

Lambeth Palace. He took me aside into a small shrubbery, and informed me that he was really a Buddhist. He added that nearly all the bishops were."

"Is it true that Mr. Haweis introduced his congregation to a Mahatma in the vestry after service last Sunday?" said Madame Valtesi. "I heard so, and that he has persuaded Little Tich to read the lessons for the rest of the season. I think it is rather hard upon the music-halls. There is really so much competition nowadays!"

"I know nothing about Mr. Haweis," said Mr. Smith, drinking some water from a wine-glass. "I understood he was a conjurer, or an entertainer, or something of that kind."

"Oh no, he is quite a clergyman," exclaimed Mrs. Windsor. "Quite; except when he is in the pulpit, of course. And then I suppose he thinks it more religious to drop it."

"Since I have been away there has been a great change in services," said Lady Locke. "They are so much brighter and more cheerful."

"Yes, Christians are getting very lively," said Madame Valtesi, helping herself to a cutlet in aspic. "They demand plenty of variety in their devotional exercises, and what Arthur Roberts, or somebody, calls short 'turns.' The most popular of all the London clergymen invariably has an anthem that lasts half-an-hour, and preaches for five minutes by a stop watch."

"I scarcely think that music should entirely oust doctrine," began Mr. Smith, refusing an entrée with a gentle wave of his hand.

"The clergyman I sit under," said Mrs. Windsor, "always stops for several minutes before his sermon, so that the people can go out if they want to."

"How inconsiderate," said Mr. Amarinth; "of course no one dares to move. English people never do dare to move, except at the wrong time. They think it is less noticeable to go out at a concert during a song than during an interval. The English labour under so many curious delusions. They think they are respectable, for instance, if they are not noticed, and that to be talked about is to be fast. Of course the really fast people are never talked about at all. Half the young men in London, whose names are bywords, are intensely and hopelessly virtuous. They know it, and that is why they look so pale. The consciousness of virtue is a terrible thing, is it not, Mr. Smith?"

"I am afraid I hardly caught what you were saying. No pudding, thank you," said that gentleman.

"I was saying that we moderns are really all much better than we seem. There is far more hypocrisy of vice nowadays than hypocrisy of virtue. The amount of excellence going about is positively quite amazing, if one only knows where to look for it; but good people in Society are so terribly afraid of being found out."

"Really! Can that be the case?"

"Indeed, it can. Society is absolutely frank about its sins, but absolutely secretive about its lapses into goodness, if I may so phrase it. I once knew a young nobleman who went twice to church on Sunday—in the morning and the afternoon. He managed to conceal it for nearly five years, but one day, to his horror, he saw a paragraph in the *Star*—the *Star* is a small evening paper which circulates chiefly among members of the Conservative party who desire to know what the aristocracy are doing—revealing his exquisite secret. He fled the country immediately, and is now living in retirement in Buenos Ayres, which is, I am told, the modern equivalent of the old-fashioned purgatory."

"Good gracious! London must be in a very sad condition," said Mr. Smith, in considerable excitement. "No, thank you, I never touch fruit. Things used to be very different, I imagine, although I have never been in town except for the day, and then merely to call upon my dentist."

"Yes, this is an era of change," murmured Lord Reggie, who had spoken little and eaten much. "Good women have taken to talking about vice, and, in no long time, bad men will take to talking about virtue."

"I think you are wronging good women, Lord Reggie," said Lady Locke, rather gravely.

"It is almost impossible to wrong a woman now," he answered pensively. "Women are so busy in wronging men, that they have no time for anything else. Sarah Grand has inaugurated the Era of women's wrongs."

"I am so afraid that she will drive poor dear Mrs. Lynn Linton mad," said Mrs. Windsor, drawing on her gloves—for she persisted in believing that the presence of Mr. Smith constituted a dinner party. "Mrs. Linton's articles are really getting so very noisy. Don't you think they rather suggest Bedlam?"

"To me they suggest nothing whatever," said Amarinth wearily. "I cannot distinguish one from another. They are all like sheep that have gone astray."

"I must say I prefer them to Lady Jeune's," said Mrs. Windsor.

"Lady Jeune catches Society by the throat and worries it," said Madame Valtesi.

"She worries it very inartistically," added Lord Reggie.

"Ah!" said Amarinth, as the ladies rose to go into the drawing-room; "she makes one great mistake. She judges of Society by her own parties, and looks at life through the spectacles of a divorce court judge. No wonder she is the bull-terrier of modern London life."

Mrs. Windsor paused at the dining-room door and looked back.

"We are going to have coffee in the garden," she said. "Will you join us there? Don't stay too long over your water, Mr. Smith?" she added, with pious archness.

"No; but I never take coffee, thank you," he answered solemnly.

VIII

SMÉ AMARINTH was generally amusing and whimsical in conversation, but, like other men, he had his special moments, and the half-hour after dinner, when the ladies, longing to remain as invisible listeners, had retired to the bald deserts of feminine society, was usually his time of triumph. His mental stays were then unfastened. He could breathe forth his stories freely. His wittiest jokes, nude, no longer clad in the shadowy garments of more or less conventional propriety, danced like bacchanals through the conversation, and kicked up heels to fire even the weary men of society. He expanded into fantastic anecdote, and mingled many a *bon mot* with the blue spirals of his mounting cigarette smoke. But to-night Mr. Smith's gentle, "I never smoke, thank you," reminded him that the fate of Lord Reggie's anthem was hanging in the balance. He resolved to tread warily among clerical prejudices, so, lighting a cigarette, and pushing the claret away from him with one plump hand, he drew his chair slowly towards Mr. Smith's, and a sweet smile spread deliberately over his rather large and intelligent face.

"I was very interested in your remark about doctrine and music at dinner," he began in his most carefully modulated voice, "and I wanted to pursue the subject a little farther, only the minds of ladies are so curious and unexpected, that I thought it better to refrain. Have you noticed that many women make a kind of profession of being shocked?"

"Surely no," said Mr. Smith, sipping his water with an inquiring air.

"Yes, positively it is so, especially if a truth about religion is uttered. They are apt to think that all truths about religion are blasphemous. It is wonderful how ready good women are to find blasphemy where it is not, and to confuse reasoning with ribaldry."

"Ah!" said the curate, looking the more ascetic because he was slightly confused in mind.

"Now you spoke of music ousting doctrine. Do you not think that the truest, the most poignant doctrine, speaks, utters itself through the arts. Music has its religion and its atheism, painting its holiness and its sin. A statue, in its white and marble stillness, may suggest to us dreams in which the angels walk, or visions that I will not characterise in the presence of an ordained priest. Even architecture may incline us to worship, and a few broken fragments of stone to faith. Have you ever been in Greece?"

"I have never been out of my own country," said Mr. Smith, "except once, when I spent a week in Wales."

"I have never made an exhaustive study of Welsh art," said Amarinth, "but I believe Mr. Gladstone thinks it gallant, while others prefer to call it little. But the point I wanted to suggest was merely this, that we can draw doctrine from the music and the painting of men, as well as from literature and sermons."

"I have never thought of it before," said Mr. Smith doubtfully.

"Mozart and Bach have given me belief that not even the subversive impotencies of Sir Arthur Sullivan, and the terribly obvious 'mysteries' of Dr. A. C. Mackenzie, have been able to take from me," murmured Lord Reggie.

"Ah! Reggie, each decade has its poet Bunn," remarked Amarinth. "We have our Bunn in Mr. Joseph Bennett, but where are his plums? Religion dwells in the arts, Mr. Smith, as irreligion so often, unhappily, lurks in the sciences."

"Indeed I have no opinion of science," the curate said with authoritative disapproval.

"Science is too often a thief. Art is a prodigal benefactor. She provides for us an almshouse in which we can take refuge when we are old and weary. And in music especially—in good music—all doctrine is crystallised. The man who has genius gathers together all his highest thoughts and aspirations, all his beliefs, his trust, his faith, and gives them forth in his art, in his music, or in his picture. Lord Reginald, for instance, would convert more men to Christianity by his exquisite and purple anthem than most preachers by all their sermons."

"Indeed, has Lord Reginald composed an anthem?" asked the curate, gazing upon Reggie with a priestly approval.

"He has, and one that Roman Catholics have delighted in. Forgive my allusion to an alien faith, but the Romanists, with all their mistakes, are not unmusical."

"I see much good in Rome," said Mr. Smith solemnly, "although it is mingled with many errors. No, not any nuts, thank you; I never touch nuts. I should like to hear this anthem."

"I could play it to you with pleasure," Reggie said, drooping his fair head slightly, "but of course it is all wrong on a piano. It requires the organ and sweet boys' voices."

"We have anthems in the church here," said Mr. Smith. "We have even done masses."

"How exquisite!" said Amarinth. "A village mass. There is something beautifully original in the notion. Ah! Mr. Smith, if your boys could have done Lord Reggie's anthem they would have learnt the doctrine of music."

"Perhaps they—would it be possible—on Sunday?" Mr. Smith said, glowing gently.

Amarinth got up, dropping his cigarette end into his finger-bowl.

"Reggie, we have found a true artist in Chenecote," he said. "Play Mr. Smith your purple notes, and I will go and take my coffee on the lawn. The moon washes the night with silver, and, thank Heaven! there are no nightingales to ruin the music of the stillness with their well-meant but ill-produced voices. Nature's songster is the worst sort of songster I know."

He walked with an ample softness into the little hall, and passed out through the French windows of the drawing-room into the shadowy garden.

On the lawn he found Lady Locke sitting alone, sipping her coffee in a basket chair. Madame Valtesi and Mrs. Windsor had strolled into the scented rose garden to discuss the inner details of a forthcoming divorce case. The murmur of their voices, uttering names of co-respondents, was faintly heard now and then as they passed up and down the tiny formal paths.

Esmé Amarinth sank down into a chair by Lady Locke and sighed heavily.

"What is the matter?" she asked.

"You have a beautiful soul," he said softly, "and I have a beautiful soul too. Why should there not be a sympathy between us? Lady Locke, I am the victim of depression. I am suffering from the malady of life. I usually have an attack of it in the morning, but it flies when the stars come out and leaves me brilliant. What can be the matter with me to-night? I ask myself the question with the most poignant anxiety, I can assure you."

She glanced at his large and solemn face, at his ample cheeks and loose mouth, and smiled slightly.

"Some circumstances have been unkind to you, perhaps?" she said.

"That could not hurt me," he answered, "for, thank Heaven! I am no philosopher, and never take facts seriously. Circumstances, my dear Lady Locke, are the lashes laid on to us by life. Some of us have to receive them with bared ivory backs, and others are permitted to keep on a coat—that is the only difference."

"Are you a pessimist?" she asked.

"I hope so. I look upon optimism as a most quaint disease, an eruption that breaks out upon the soul, and destroys all its interest, all its beauty. The optimist dresses up the amazing figures of life like Dresden shepherds and shepherdesses, and pipes a foolish tune—the Old Hundredth, or some such thing—for them to dance to. We cannot all refuse to see anything but comic opera peasants around us."

"Yet we need not replace them with pantomime demons."

"Demons, as you call them, are much more interesting. Nothing is so unattractive as goodness, except, perhaps, a sane mind in a sane body. Even the children find the fairies monotonous, I believe. An eternal smile is much more wearisome than a perpetual frown. The one sweeps away all possibilities, the other suggests a thousand."

"Every one of them sinister."

"Why not? Where would be the drama without the crime? The clash of swords is the music of the world. People talk so much to me about the beauty of confidence. They seem to entirely ignore the much more subtle beauty of doubt. To believe is very dull. To doubt is intensely engrossing. The Apostle Thomas was artistic up to a certain point. He appreciated the value of shadows in a picture. To be on the alert is to live. To be lulled into security is to die."

"But if you pushed that amusing theory to its limits you would arrive at the contradiction in terms—to be happy is to be miserable."

"Certainly. To be what is commonly called happy is a mental complaint demanding careful treatment. The happy people of the world have their value, but only the negative value of foils. They throw up and emphasise the beauty, and the fascination of the unhappy. Scarlet and black are the finest of all the colours. And to cease to doubt is to despair—for a really talented man or woman. That is why people become sceptics. They desire to save themselves from intellectual annihilation."

"Yet the mental pleasure of proving a case may be keen."

"But it cannot be lasting. You do not see the delight that must attend upon conjecture. Let me put it to you in another way. Can you conceive loving a man whom you felt you understood?"

"Certainly. Especially if he were difficult for other people to understand."

"Ah! you begin to appreciate the value of doubt. We often begin by desiring others to enjoy what we shall eventually want for ourselves. The moment we understand a human being, our love for that human being spreads his wings preparatory to flying out of the window."

Lady Locke, who had begun to look earnest, seemed to recollect herself with an effort, and dispelled the gravity that was settling over her face with a smile.

"You go very far in your admirable desire to amuse," she said.

"I think not," he answered, putting down his cup with an elaborate serenity. "One must perpetually doubt to be faithful. Perplexity and mistrust fan affection into passion, and so bring about those beautiful tragedies that alone make life worth living. Women once felt this while men did not, and so women once ruled the world. But men are awakening from their mental slumber, and are becoming incomprehensible. Lord Reggie is an instance of what I mean. The average person finds him exquisitely difficult to comprehend. He fascinates by being sedulously unexpected. Listen to his anthem. He is beginning to play it. How unexpected it is. It always does what the ear wants, and all modern music does what the ear does not want. Therefore the ear always expects to be disappointed, and Lord Reggie astonishes it by never disappointing it."

The faint music of the piano now tinkled out into the night, and numerous simple harmonies and full closes fell melodiously upon their hearing.

"Lord Reggie is certainly very unlike his anthem," said Lady Locke, listening a little sadly.

"Reggie is unlike everything except himself. He is completely wonderful, and wonderfully complete. He lives for sensations, while other people live for faiths, or for convictions, or for prejudices. He would make any woman unhappy. How beautiful!"

"Is it always a sign of intelligence to be what others are not?"

But she received no direct answer to her question, for at this moment Madame Valtesi and Mrs. Windsor came to them across the lawn. They had finished trying the divorce case.

"What is that about intelligence?" Madame Valtesi asked croakily.

"Dear lady!" said Esmé, getting up out of his chair slowly, "intelligence is the demon of our age. Mine bores me horribly. I am always trying to find a remedy for it. I have experimented with absinthe, but gained no result. I have read the collected works of Walter Besant. They are said to sap the mental powers. They did not sap mine. Opium has proved useless, and green tea cigarettes leave me positively brilliant. What am I to do? I so long for the lethargy, the sweet peace of stupidity. If only I were Lewis Morris!"

"Unfortunate man! You should treat your complaint with the knife. Become a popular author."

She laughed without smiling, an uncanny habit of hers, and turned to the window.

"I hear Mr. Smith saying that he must go," she said.

Mrs. Windsor rustled forward to speed the parting guest.

That night Esmé said to Reggie in the smoking-room—

"Reggie, Lady Locke will marry you if you ask her."

"I suppose so," the boy said.

"Shall you ask her?"

"I suppose so. Mr. Smith is going to do my anthem on Sunday."

They lit their cigarettes.

IX

OTHER," said Tommy, with exceeding great frankness, "I love Lord Reggie."

"My dear boy," Lady Locke said, "what a sudden affection! Why, to-day is only Friday, and you never met him until Wednesday. That is quick work."

"It's very easy," answered Tommy. "It doesn't take any time. Why should it?"

"Well, we generally get to like people very much gradually. We find out what they are by degrees, and consider whether they are worth caring for."

"I don't," said Tommy. "Directly he came to play ball with me I loved him. Why shouldn't I?"

"Tommy, you are very direct," his mother cried, laughing. "Now you have finished your breakfast, run out into the garden. I heard Mr. Smith's boys just now. I expect they are in the paddock."

"Athanasius doesn't play cricket badly," Tommy remarked meditatively, "only he caught a ball once on his spectacles. Lord Reggie would never have done that."

"Lord Reggie doesn't wear spectacles," said his mother.

Tommy looked at her seriously for a minute, as if he were taking in the relevance of this contention. Then he said—

"No, he's not such a bunger," and dashed off towards the paddock.

"Where does he get those words?" thought Lady Locke to herself, preparing to go to her own breakfast.

She found Lord Reggie alone in the room reading his letters. He was dressed in loose white flannel, and in the buttonhole of his thin jacket a big green carnation was stuck. It looked perfectly fresh.

"How do you manage to keep that flower alive so long?" asked Lady Locke, as they sat down opposite to one another. For there was no formality at this meal, and people began just when they felt inclined.

"I don't understand," Reggie answered, looking at her across his mushrooms.

"Why, you have worn it for two days already."

"This? No. Esmé and I have some sent down every morning from a florist's in Covent Garden."

"Really! Is it worth while?"

"I think that sort of thing is the only sort of thing that is worth while. Most people are utterly wrong, they worship what they call great things. I worship little details. This flower is a detail. I worship it."

"Do you regard it as an emblem, then?"

"No. I hate emblems. The very word makes one think of mourning rings, and everlasting flowers, and urns, and mementoes of all sorts. Why are people so afraid of forgetting? There is nothing more beautiful than to forget, except, perhaps, to be forgotten. I wear this flower because its colour is exquisite. I have no other reason."

"But its colour is not natural."

"Not yet. Nature has not followed art so far. She always requires time. Esmé invented this flower two months ago. Only a few people wear it, those who are followers of the higher philosophy."

"The higher philosophy! What is that?"

"The philosophy to be afraid of nothing, to dare to live as one wishes to live, not as the middle-classes wish one to live; to have the courage of one's desires, instead of only the cowardice of other people's."

"Mr. Amarinth is the high priest of this philosophy, I suppose?"

"Esmé is the bravest man I know," said Reggie, taking some marmalade. "I think sometimes that he sins even more perfectly than I do. He is so varied. And he escapes those absurd things, consequences. His sin always finds him out. He is never at home to it by any chance. Why do you look at me so strangely?"

"Do I look at you strangely?" she asked, with a sudden curious nervousness. "Perhaps it is because you are so strange, so unlike the men whom I have been accustomed to. Your aims are different from theirs."

"That is impossible, Lady Locke."

"Impossible! Why?"

"Because I have no aims; I have only emotions. If we live for aims we blunt our emotions. If we live for aims, we live for one minute, for one day, for one year, instead of for every minute, every day, every year. The moods of one's life are life's beauties. To yield to all one's moods is to really live."

Mrs. Windsor's voice was heard outside at this moment, and Lady Locke put her napkin down upon the cloth and got up. In performing this action she left her hand on the table for an instant. Lord Reggie touched it with his. She immediately drew her hand away, and her face reddened slightly. But she said nothing, and went quietly out of the room.

Mrs. Windsor was outside speaking to one of the tall footmen. When she saw her cousin she jingled her keys languidly and smiled.

"Good morning, darling," she said. "I am arranging about the choir practice to-night. We are going to entertain all the dear little choir-boys to supper afterwards, and they will sing catches, and so on, so delicious by moonlight. Mr. Amarinth has invented a new catch for them. And on Monday the school-children are coming to tea on the lawn, and games. Mr. Amarinth says that charity always begins abroad, but one couldn't have a school treat in Belgrave Square, could one? It would be quite sacrilege, or bad form, which is worse. We must try and invent some new games. You and Lord Reggie must put your heads together."

"Thank you, Betty," Lady Locke said, moving rather hastily on towards the garden. Mrs. Windsor looked after her with the sudden sly suspicion of a stupid woman who fancies she is being discerning and clever.

"Something has happened," she thought. "Can Reggie have said anything already?"

She walked into the breakfast-room, where she found Lord Reggie alone.

He was holding up a table-spoon filled with marmalade to catch the light from a stray sunbeam that filtered in through the drawn blinds, and wore a rapt look, a "caught-up" look, as Mrs. Windsor would have expressed it.

"Good morning," he said softly. "Is not this marmalade Godlike? This marvellous, clear, amber glow, amber with a touch of red in it, almost makes me believe in an after life. Surely, surely marmalade can never die!"

"I must have been mistaken," Mrs. Windsor thought, as she expressed her sense of the eternity of jams in general in suitable language.

Meanwhile Lady Locke had gone into the garden. The weather was quite perfect. England seemed to have made a special effort, and to have determined to show what she could do in the way of a summer. The sky had been well swept of clouds, and shimmered in the heat almost as if it had been varnished. The garden was revelling in the growing luxury of warmth. It never looked parched, Mrs. Windsor's gardeners were too agile with the hose for that. The hundreds of roses were letting out their perfume shyly, as pretty children let out their secrets. The carnations nodded to one another against the stone wall that was clothed with Espalier pear trees. The great cedar tree spread its arms out to catch the soft warm breeze in its embrace. Over the tree-tops the swallows were circling with their little characteristic air of discreet and graceful frivolity. Tennyson would doubtless have addressed them. Lady Locke did not even notice them. She was thinking, and too deeply to sit down.

She was in that strange condition of mind that is called being angry with oneself. A miniature civil war was raging within her, in which two mental voices abused one another, and asked one another the most strangely impertinent and inappropriate questions.

One said, "What on earth are you about?"

The other, "You have no right to ask. Mind your own business."

"You are letting yourself go in a way that is humiliating."

"Indeed, I am doing nothing of the kind."

"Why did you blush, then, when he merely touched your hand? He is simply a thoughtless, foolish boy."

"I shan't talk to you any more."

But still the urgent conversation went on within. Lady Locke was, in fact, very angry with herself, and considerably surprised at her own girlishness. For that was what she called it, for want of a better name. She was half disgusted at finding herself so young. Had life done nothing more for her than this? Was she still liable to become an easy prey to emotions that were undignified and inappropriate? It seemed as if her heart were clouded while her mind remained clear, for she saw Lord Reggie quite as he was, and yet she began to like him quite absurdly. Why she was attracted by him she could not conceive. Was it the swing of Nature's pendulum? She had loved a hard, brusque man, and had found a certain satisfaction in his blunt and not too considerate affection; now she found something interesting in a nature that seemed boyish to softness, that was no doubt full of absurdity, that was, so people said, and he himself boasted, given over to vice, to the tasting of emotions that is unfortunately so dangerous, often so inhuman in its humanity. Perhaps it was really Lord Reggie's personal beauty or prettiness that attracted her, for, say what one will, a pretty boy steps easily into the good graces of even a strong-natured woman. Perhaps it was his fleeting air of weakness combined with daring that drew her to him. She could not tell. She only knew, as she walked among the shy roses, that the casual touch of his hand—a hand, too, that was very like a girl's—had communicated to her quite a startlingly strong emotion. Alas! the motherly feeling seemed to have had its little day, and to have been swept off the stage on which her mental drama was being acted. It had played a principal part, but now an understudy appeared, more full-blooded, stronger, wilder. Lady Locke was very angry with herself among the roses that morning.

She knew she was a fool, but she knew also that she had no intention of making a fool of herself. She had too much character, too much observation, both of others and of herself, to do that.

Madame Valtesi joined her presently, leaning on her cane and fanning herself rather languidly.

"Nature has gone into quite a vulgar extreme to-day," she said. "It is distinctly too hot for propriety. One wants to sit about in one's skeleton. I wonder what Mr. Amarinth's skeleton would be like— not quite nice, I fancy. I have had bad news by the post."

"Indeed! I am sorry."

"My dearest enemy has written to say that she is going to marry again. I did not wish her so much ill as that. It is really curious. If some people have been chastised with whips, they pine after scorpions. Women have such an unwholesome craving to experience the keenest edge of pain, that I believe many of them would cut themselves with knives, like the priests of Baal, if they could not get a husband to perform the operation for them."

"You speak rather bitterly of your sex."

"Do I? A nineteenth-century cynic minus vitriol would be like a goose minus sage and onions. I prefer to be a goose with those alleviations of the goose nature. My enemy married for money the first time, now she is going in for celebrity. The chief drawback to celebrity is that it is generally dressed in mourning; a kind of half mourning when it is notoriety only, and absolute weeds when it is fame. Why should cleverness and crape go together? People are so frightfully solemn when they have made a name, that it is like doing a term of hard labour to be with them for five minutes. Stupidity gives you a ticket-of-leave, and sheer foolish ignorance is complete emancipation, without even police supervision."

"I suppose it is always difficult not to take oneself seriously?"

"I do not find it so. My mental proceedings generally strike me as the best joke I know, a sort of Moore and Burgess performance, with corner men always asking riddles that nobody can ever answer. Mr. Amarinth is taking himself seriously this morning. He is composing a catch for the choir-boys to sing to-night after supper. It is to be parody, or, as he calls it, an elevation of 'Three Blind Mice,' and is to be about youth and life. It ought to be amusing."

"Mr. Amarinth is generally amusing."

"Yes, he has got hold of a good recipe for making the world laugh and think him clever. The only mistake he makes is, that he sometimes serves up only the recipe, and omits the dish that ought to be the result of it altogether. One cannot dine off a recipe, however good and ingenious it may be. It is like reading a guide-book at home instead of travelling. Dear me, it is too hot! I shall go and lie down and read Oscar Wilde's 'Decay of Lying.' That always sends me to sleep. It is like himself, all artfulness and no art."

She strolled languidly away, still fanning herself.

Esmé Amarinth and Lord Reggie were busy at the piano, inventing and composing the elevation of "Three Blind Mice."

Lady Locke could hear an odd little primitive sort of tune, and then their voices singing, one after the other, some words. She could only catch a few.

> "Rose—white—youth,
> Rose—white—youth,
> Rose—white—youth,"

sang Lord Reggie's clear, but rather thin voice. Then Amarinth broke in with a deeper note, and words were lost.

Lady Locke listened for a moment. Then she suddenly turned and went out of the garden. She made her way to the paddock, and spent the rest of the morning in playing cricket with her boy and the curate's children. She caught three people out, made twenty-five runs, and began to feel quite healthy-minded and cheerful again.

X

HOIR-BOYS at a distance in their surplices are generally charming. Choir-boys close by in mundane suits, bought at a cheap tailor's, or sewed together at home, are not always so attractive. The cherubs' wings with which imagination has endowed them drop off, and they subside into cheeky, and sometimes scrubby, little boys, with a tendency towards peppermints, and a strong bias in favour of slang and tricks. The choir-boys of Chenecote, however, had been well trained under Mr. Smith's ascetic eye; and though he had not drained the humanity entirely out of them, he had persuaded them to perfect cleanliness, if not to perfect godliness. They appeared at Mrs. Windsor's cottage that evening in an amazing condition of shiny rosiness, with round cheeks that seemed to focus the dying rays of the setting sun, and hair brushed perfectly flat to their little bullet-shaped heads, in which the brains worked with much excitement and anticipation. Their eyes were mostly blue and innocent, and they were all afflicted with a sort of springy shyness which led them at one moment to jumps of joy, and at another to blushes and smiling speechlessness. They were altogether naïve and invigorating, and even Madame Valtesi, peering at them through her tortoise-shell eyeglass, was moved to a dry approbation. She nodded her head at them two or three times, and remarked—

"Boys are much nicer than girls. They giggle less, and smile more. In surplices these would be quite fetching—quite."

Mrs. Windsor, too, was quite desolated by the fact that they had not come in what she persisted in calling their little nightgowns. She expressed her sorrow to the head boy, who occasionally sang "Oh! for the wings of a dove!" as a solo at evensong, and was consequently looked up to with deep respect by all the village.

"I thought you always wore them when you sang!" she said plaintively. "It makes it so much more impressive. Couldn't you send for them?"

The head boy, who was just twelve, blushed violently, and said he was afraid Mr. Smith would be angry. They were kept for the church. Mr. Smith was very particular, he added.

"How absurd the clergy are!" murmured Mrs. Windsor aside to Esmé Amarinth. "Making such a fuss about a few nightgowns. But perhaps they are blessed, or consecrated, or something, and that makes them different. Well, it can't be helped, but I did think they would look so pretty standing in the moonlight after supper and singing catches in them—like the angels, you know."

"Do the angels sing catches after supper?" Madame Valtesi asked of Lady Locke, who was trying to restrain the pardonable excitement of Tommy. "I am so ignorant about these things."

Lady Locke did not hear. She was watching the rather fussy movements of Lord Reggie, who was darting about, sorting out the copies of his anthem, which the village organist had laboriously written out that day. His face was pale, and his eyes shone with eagerness.

"After all," Lady Locke thought, "he is very young, and has a good deal of freshness left in him. To-night, even among these boys, he looks like a boy."

The choir were quite fascinated by him. Most of them had never seen a lord before, and his curious fair beauty vaguely appealed to their boyish hearts. Then the green carnation that he wore in his evening coat created a great amazement in their minds. They stared upon it with round eyes, scarcely certain that it could be a flower at all. Jimmy Sands, the head boy, was specially magnetised by it. It appeared to mesmerise him, and to render him unaware of outward things. Whenever it moved his eyes moved too, and he even forgot to blush as he lost himself in its astonishing green fascinations.

"How exquisite rose-coloured youth is," Amarinth said softly to Mrs. Windsor, as Lord Reggie ranged the little boys before him, and prepared to strike a chord upon the piano. "There is nothing in the world worth having except youth, youth with its perfect sins, sins with the dew upon them like red roses—youth with its purple passions and its wild and wonderful tears. The world worships youth, for the world is very old and grey and weary, and the world is becoming very respectable, like a man who is too decrepit to sin. Ah, dear friend, let us sin while we may, for the time will come when we shall be able to sin no more. Why, why do the young neglect their passionate pulsating opportunities?"

He sighed, as the wind sighs through the golden strings of a harp, musically, pathetically. These little chorister boys made him feel that his youth had slipped from him, and left him alone with his intellect and his epigrams. Sometimes he shivered with cold among those epigrams. He was tired of them. He knew them so well, and then so many of them had foreign blood in their veins, and were inclined to taunt him with being English. Ah! youth with its simple puns and its full-blooded pleasures, when there is no gold dust in the hair and no wrinkles about the eyes, when the sources of an epigram, like the sources of the Nile, are undiscoverable, and the joy of being led into sin has not lost its pearly freshness! Ah! youth—youth! He sighed, and sighed again, for he thought his sigh as beautiful as the face of a young Greek god!

"Sing it daintily!" cried Lord Reggie, playing the spinet-like prelude with the soft pedal down, "Let it tinkle."

And the little rosy boys tried to let it, squeaking wrong notes with all their might and main, and fixing their eyes upon Lord Reggie and his carnation, rather than upon their sheets of music.

"Thy lips are like a thread, like a thre-ead o-of scar-let, and thy speech, thy spee-eech i-is come-ly," they squealed at the top of their village voices, strong in the possession of complete unmusicalness. And Lord Reggie wandered about over the piano, holding his fair head on one side, and smiling upon them with his pale blue eyes. He trusted rather in repetition than in correction, and eliminated the wrong notes gradually by dint of playing the right ones himself over and over again.

After hearing his anthem about five minutes, Mrs. Windsor and her guests adjourned to the garden, leaving Tommy Locke seated on the music stool by Lord Reggie's side, gazing at him with excited adoration, and joining in the chorus with all his might.

Amarinth accompanied Lady Locke.

"Thy lips are like a thread of scarlet," he murmured, "like a thread of scarlet. Solomon must have lived a very beautiful life. He understood the art of life, the magic of moods. Why do we not all live for our own sensations, instead of for other people? Why do we consider the world at all? The world taken *en masse* is a monster, crammed with prejudices, packed with prepossessions, cankered with what it calls virtues, a puritan, a prig. And the art of life is the art of defiance. To defy. That is what we ought to live for, instead of living, as we do, to acquiesce. The world divides actions into three classes: good actions, bad actions that you may do, and bad actions that you may not do. If you stick to the good actions, you are respected by the good. If you stick to the bad actions that you may do, you are respected by the bad. But if you perform the bad actions that no one may do, then the good and the bad set upon you, and you are lost indeed. How I hate that word natural."

"Why? I think it is one of the most beautiful of words."

"How strange! To me it means all that is middle-class, all that is of the essence of jingoism, all that is colourless, and without form, and void. It might be a beautiful word, but it is the most debased coin in the currency of language. Certain things are classed as natural, and certain things are classed as unnatural—for all the people born into the world. Individualism is not allowed to enter into the matter. A child is unnatural if it hates its mother. A mother is unnatural if she does not wish to have children. A man is unnatural if he never falls in love with a woman. A boy is unnatural if he prefers looking at pictures to playing cricket, or dreaming over the white naked beauty of a Greek statue to a game of football under Rugby rules. If our virtues are not cut on a pattern, they are unnatural. If our vices are not according to rule, they are unnatural. We must be good naturally. We must sin naturally. We must live naturally, and die naturally. Branwell Brontë died standing up, and the world has looked upon him as a blasphemer ever since. Why must we stand up to live, and lie down to die? Byron had a club foot in his mind, and so Byron is a byword. Yet twisted minds are as natural to some people as twisted bodies. It is natural to one man to live like Charles Kingsley, to preach gentleness, and love sport; it is natural to another to dream away his life on the narrow couch of an opium den, with his head between a fellow-sinner's feet. I love what are called warped minds, and deformed natures, just as I love the long necks of Burne-Jones' women, and the faded rose-leaf beauty of Walter Pater's unnatural prose. Nature is generally purely vulgar, just as many women are vulgarly pure. There are only a few people in the world who dare to defy the grotesque code of rules that has been drawn up by that fashionable mother, Nature, and they defy—as many women drink, and many men are vicious —in secret, with the door locked and the key in their pockets. And what is life to them? They can always hear the footsteps of the detective in the street outside."

"Society must have its police while Society has its criminals," said Lady Locke, a little warmly.

"Yes. The person who is called a 'copper,' because you can only bribe him with silver, or with gold."

"I think it is essentially a question of the preponderance of numbers," she added more quietly. "Warped and twisted minds are in the minority. If more than half the world had club feet, we should not think the club-footed man a cripple."

"Ah! that is just the mistake that every one makes nowadays. Unnatural minds are far more common, and therefore, according to the middle-class view, more natural than people choose to suppose. I believe that the tyranny of minorities is the plague that we suffer under. How intensely interesting it would be to take a census of vices. Why should we take infinite trouble to find out how old we are. Age is a question of temperament, just as youth is a question of health. We are not interesting because of what we are, but because of what we do."

"But we reveal what we are by our acts."

Esmé Amarinth looked at her with surprised compassion.

"Forgive me," he said. "That is a curious old fallacy that lingers among us like an old faith, unable to get away from people's minds because it has literally not a leg to stand upon, or to walk with. We reveal what we are not by our acts."

"How can that be? By our words. Surely that is what you mean?"

"No, we lie in deed perpetually. That is what makes life so curious, and sometimes so interesting. We lie to the world in open deeds, to ourselves in secret deeds. We have a beautiful passion for all that is theatrical, and we have two kinds of plays in which we indulge our desire of mumming, the plays that we act for others, and the plays that we act for ourselves. Both are interesting, but the latter are engrossing. Our secret virtues, our secret vices, are the plays that we act for our own benefit. Both are equally selfish, and bizarre, and full of imagination. We make vices of our virtues, and virtues of our vices. The former we consider the duty that we owe to others, the latter the duty that we owe to ourselves. If we practise the latter with the greatest earnestness, are stricter about the rehearsals, in fact, it is not wonderful."

"But then, if you explain everything away like that, there is no residuum left. Where is the reality? Where is the real man?"

Mr. Amarinth smiled with a wide sweetness.

"The real man is a Mrs. Harris," he replied. "There is, believe me, 'no sich a person.'"

"But really that is absurd," Lady Locke said. "There must be an ego somewhere."

"If there were, should we not learn a permanent means of satisfying it? We are always sending out actions to knock upon its door, and the answer is always—Not at home. Then we send out other actions of a different kind. We knock in all sorts of various ways. Yet 'Not at home' is always the answer."

Lady Locke looked at him with a distaste that she could scarcely conceal.

"You are very amusing," she said bluntly. "But you are not very satisfactory. I wonder if you have a philosophy of life?"

"I have," he said, "a beautiful one."

"What is it?"

"Take everything—and nothing seriously. And in your career of deception always, if possible, include yourself among those whom you deceive."

"Esmé! Esmé!" cried Lord Reggie's petulant boyish voice. "Where are you? We have finished the practice, and Mrs. Windsor wants us to come in to supper. Oh! here you are. Lady Locke, the boys say they like my anthem. Jimmy thinks it is beautiful. Isn't he a dear boy?"

"Does *he* include himself among those whom he deceives?" she thought, as they walked towards the house.

The two tall footmen, more rigidly supercilious in their powdered hair than ever, were already ranging the ecstatic and amazed little choir-boys in their seats. Tables had been placed in horse-shoe fashion, and in the centre of the horse-shoe Mrs. Windsor took her seat, with Mr. Smith, who had just arrived, Madame Valtesi, and Lady Locke. Lord Reggie and Esmé Amarinth sat among the boys at the ends of the two sides of the horse-shoe. Tommy was on Lord Reggie's right hand. The tall footmen moved noiselessly about handing the various dishes, but at first a difficulty presented itself. Jimmy Sands was far too nervous to accept any food from the gorgeous flunkeys. He started violently and blushed most prettily whenever they came near him. But he shook his head shyly at the dishes, and as all the other boys followed his lead, the supper at first threatened to be a failure. It was not until Mr. Smith went round personally putting chicken and *foie gras* and other delights upon their plates, that they found courage to fall to, and then they were much too shy to talk. With their heads held well over their food they gobbled mutely, occasionally shooting side glances at one another and at their entertainers, and watching furtively with a view of discovering whether they were doing the right thing.

Mrs. Windsor found them most refreshing.

"How sweet innocence is!" she languidly ejaculated, as she saw little Tim Wright, a fair baby of eight, drop a large truffle head downwards into his lap. "We Londoners pay for our pleasures, Mr. Smith, I can assure you. We lose our freshness. We are not like happy choir-boys."

That Mrs. Windsor was quite unlike a happy choir-boy was fairly obvious. Her fringed yellow hair, her tired, got-up eyes, her powdered cheeks, betrayed her a *mondaine*. She was indeed an acute and bizarre contrast to the troop of shyly enchanted children by whom she was surrounded. But Mr. Amarinth looked even more out of place than she did, although he was, as always, tremendously at his ease. His large and sleek body towered up at the end of the long table. His carefully crimped head was smilingly bowed to catch the whispered confidences of Jimmy Sands, and the green carnation, staring from the lapel of his evening coat, seemed to watch with a bristling amazement the homely diversions of an unaccustomed rusticity.

The little boys were all hopelessly in love with Lord Reggie, to whom they had learnt, over the anthem, to draw near with a certain confidence, but they gazed upon Amarinth with an awe that made their bosoms heave, and could not reply to his remarks without drawing in their breath at the same time—a circumstance which rendered their artless communications less lucidly audible than might have been desired. Amarinth, however, was serenely gracious, and might be heard conversing about rustic joys and the charms of the country in a way that would have done every credit to Virgil. Lady Locke could not resist listening to his rather loud voice, and the fragments she heard amused her greatly. At one moment he was hymning the raptures of bee-keeping, at another letting off epigrams on the fascinating subject of hay-making.

"Ah! dear boy," she heard him saying to the ingenuous Jimmy, "cling to your youth! Cling to the haytime of your life, ere the fields are bare, and all the emotions are stacked away for fear of the rain. There is nothing like rose-pure youth, Jimmy. One day your round cheeks will grow raddled, the light will fade from your brown eyes, and the scarlet from your lips. You will become feeble and bloated and inane—a shivering satyr with a soul of lead. The sirens will sing to you, and you will not hear them. The shepherds will pipe to you, and you will not dance. The flocks will go forth to feed, and the harvests will be sown and gathered in, and the voice of the green summer will chant among the red and the yellow roses, and the serenades of the bees will make musical the scented air. By the ruined, moss-clothed barn the owl will build her nest, and the twilight will tread a measure with the night. And the rustic maidens will gather the shell-pink honeysuckle with their lovers, and the amorous clouds will slumber above the exquisite plough-boy with his primrose locks, as he wanders, whistling, on his way. Nature, inartistic, monotonous Nature, will renew the sap of her youth, and the dewy freshness of her first pale springtime, but the sap of your youth will have run dry for ever, and the voice of your springtime will be mute and toneless. Ah, Jimmy, Jimmy! cling to your youth!"

Jimmy looked painfully embarrassed, and helped himself to some pickled walnuts which one of the tall footmen handed to him at that moment. Mrs. Windsor had a vague idea that all poor people lived upon pickles, and she had commanded her housekeeper to lay in a large store of them for this occasion. Having landed them safely upon his plate, Jimmy proceeded to devour them, helping himself to some cold beef as a species of condiment, and keeping an amazed eye all the time upon Amarinth, who surveyed the horse-shoe table with a glance of comfortable and witty superiority.

"I have composed a catch, Jimmy," he proceeded, "a beautiful rainbow catch, which we will flute presently in the moonlight. Do you know 'Three Blind Mice'?"

"Yes, sir," answered Jimmy, with a sudden smile of radiant understanding, while the little boys nearest leaned their round heads forward, happy in hearing an expression which they could well understand.

"How beautiful it is in its simplicity! My catch is even simpler and more beautiful. We will sing it, Jimmy, as no nightingales could ever sing it. Take some more of those walnuts. Their rich mahogany colour reminds me of the background of a picture by Velasquez."

Jimmy took some more with wondering acquiescence, and Amarinth leaned back negligently peeling a peach, and smiling—as if, having begun to smile, he had fallen into a reverie and forgotten to stop.

Madame Valtesi was a little bored. Youth did not appeal to her at all, except in young men, of whom she was pertinaciously fond. As to small boys, she considered them an evil against which somebody ought to legislate. These small boys, though they had been slow in beginning to eat, were slower still in finishing. Their appetites seemed to grow gradually, but continuously, with what they fed upon, and it was impossible for the tall footmen to take them unawares and remove their plates, having regard to the fact that, as they never spoke, they were always steadily eating. The feast seemed interminable.

"I am afraid they will all be very seedy to-morrow," she croaked to Mr. Smith, whose asceticism seemed to have been left at home on this occasion. "Surely they are bursting by this time."

"I trust not," he replied; "I sincerely trust not. Much food late at night is certainly imprudent, but really I have not the heart to stop them."

"But they will never stop. I believe they think it would be bad manners."

Mr. Smith cast his eyes round, and, observing that the little boys' faces were considerably flushed, and that an air of mere gourmandising had decidedly set in, suddenly became ascetic again. After making certain that all the people of the house had finished, he therefore abruptly rose to his feet, knocked upon the table with the handle of a knife, and muttered a rapid and unintelligible High Church grace. The effect of this was astonishing. A tableau ensued, in which the mouths of all the performers were seen to be wide open for at least half a minute, while spoons full of pudding, or fruit, were lifted towards them, and the round eyes above them were focussed with a concentration of complete surprise and agitation upon the intermittent clergyman, who had sat down again, and was speaking to Mrs. Windsor about chasubles. Then, as at a signal, all the spoons, still full, were pensively returned to the plates, and an audible sigh stole softly round the room. The gates of Paradise were swinging to.

Mrs. Windsor rose, and said, as she went out, to Mr. Amarinth—

"Do teach them your catch now. We will go into the garden. If only they had on their nightgowns? It is such a disappointment."

In the garden, which was rather dark, for the moon had not yet fully risen, Lady Locke found Lord Reggie standing by her side with

Tommy, who had formed a passionate attachment to him, and showed it violently both in words and deeds.

"Let us sit down here," he said, drawing forward a chair for her. "Esmé wants me to hear his music from a distance. Tommy, you go in and sing. We want to listen to you."

Tommy ran off excitedly.

Lady Locke and Lord Reggie sat down silently. A few yards away Mrs. Windsor, Madame Valtesi, and Mr. Smith formed a heterogeneous and singularly inappropriate group. Through the lighted windows of the drawing-room a multitude of bobbing small heads might be discerned, and the large form of Esmé Amarinth in the act of reciting the words of his catch.

Lord Reggie looked at Lady Locke, and sighed softly.

"Why are beautiful things so sad?" he said. "This night is like some exquisite dark youth full of sorrow. If you listen, you can hear the murmur of his grief in the wind. It is as if he had shed tears, and known renunciations."

"We all know renunciations," she answered. "And they are sad, but they are great too. We are often greatest when we give something up."

"I think renunciations are foolish," he said. "I only once gave up a pleasure, and the remembrance of it has haunted me like a grey ghost ever since. Why do people think it an act of holiness to starve their souls? We are here to express ourselves, not to fast twice in a week. Yet how few men and women ever dare to express themselves fully?"

Lady Locke looked up, and seemed to come to a sudden resolution.

"Do you ever express your real self by what you say or do?" she asked.

"Yes, always nearly."

"Even by wearing that green carnation?"

There was a ring of earnestness in her voice that evidently surprised him a little.

"Because," she went on, speaking more rapidly, "I take that as a symbol. I cannot help it. It seems like the motto of your life, and it is a tainted motto. Why—"

But at this moment a delicate sound of "Sh-sh!" came from Mrs. Windsor, and the voice of Jimmy Sands, an uncertain treble with a quaver in it, was heard singing Esmé Amarinth's catch. He sang it right through before the other circling voices rippled in—

> "Rose-white youth,
> Pas-sionate, pale,
> A singing stream in a silent vale,
> A fairy prince in a prosy tale,
> Ah! there's nothing in life so finely frail
> As rose-white youth."

"Rose-white youth," chimed the other voices, one upon one, until the air of the night throbbed with the words, and they seemed to wander away among the sleeping pageant of the flowers, away to the burnished golden disc of the slowly ascending moon.

Lord Reggie, with his fair head bent, listened with a smile on his lips, a smile in his grey blue eyes, and Lady Locke watched him and listened too, and thought of his youth and of all he was doing with it, as a sensitive, deep-hearted woman will.

And the shrill voices wound on and on, and, at last, detaching themselves one by one from the melodic fabric in which they were enmeshed, slipped into silence.

Then Mrs. Windsor spoke aloud and plaintively—

"How exquisite!" she said. "If only they had had on their little nightgowns!"

And Mr. Smith was shocked.

XI

ORD REGGIE had quite made up his mind to ask Lady Locke to marry him. He didn't in the least wish to be married, and felt that he never should. But he also felt that marriage did not matter much either way. In modern days it is a contract of no importance, as Esmé Amarinth often said, and therefore a contract that can be entered into without searching of heart or loss of perfect liberty. To him it simply meant that a good-natured woman, who liked to kiss him, would open an account for him at her banker's, and let him live with her when he felt so disposed. He considered that such an arrangement would not be a bad one, especially as the good-natured woman would in course of time cease to like kissing him, and so free him from the one awkwardness that walked in the train of matrimony. He told Esmé Amarinth of his decision.

Esmé sighed.

"So you are to be a capitalist, Reggie," he said. "Will you sing in the woods near Esher? Will you flute to the great god whom stockbrokers vulgarly worship? I wonder what a stockbroker is like. I don't think I have ever seen one. I go out in Society too much, I suppose. Society has its drawbacks. You meet so few people in it nowadays, and Royalties are of course strictly tabooed. I was dining with Lady Murray last week, and mentioned the Prince by mistake. She got quite red all down her neck, and snorted—you know how she snorts, as if she had been born a Baroness!—'One must draw the line somewhere.' The old aristocracy draws it at Princes now, and who can blame them. Vulgarity has become so common that it has lost its charm, and I shall really not be surprised if good manners and chivalry come into vogue again. How strange it will feel being polite once more, like wearing a long curled wig, and making a leg and carrying a sword. You would look perfectly charming in a wig, Reggie, and a cloak of carnation velvet with rosy shadows in the folds. You would wear it beautifully, as you wear your sins, floating negligently over your shoulders. Yes, you will be a strange and unique capitalist. The average capitalist has the face of a Gentile, and the stupidity of a Jew. I wonder how the fallacy that the Jews are a clever race grew up? It is not the man who makes money that is clever, it is the man who spends it. The intelligent pauper is the real genius. I am an intelligent pauper."

"You are marvellous, Esmé. You are like some heavy scent that hangs in clouds upon the air. You make people aware of you, who have never seen you, or read you. You are like a fifth element."

"What shall I give you for a wedding present, Reggie? I think I will give you the book of Common Prayer in the vulgar tongue. One would think it was something written by a realist. The adjectives would apply to the productions of George Moore, which are boycotted by Smith on account of their want of style or something of the sort. If George Moore could only learn the subtle art of indecency he might be tolerable. As it is, he is, like Miss Yonge, merely tedious and domesticated. He ought to associate more with educated people, instead of going perpetually to the dependent performances of the independent theatre, whose motto seems to be, 'If I don't shock you, I'm a Dutchman!' How curiously archaic it must feel to be a Dutchman. It must be like having been born in Iceland, or educated at a grammar-school. I would give almost anything to feel really Dutch for half-an-hour."

Reggie was looking a little pensive. The performance of his anthem on the morrow weighed slightly upon his mind. He had an uneasy feeling that Jimmy Sands and his followers would throw nuances to the winds when they found themselves in the public eye. When the critical morning was over he meant to propose to Lady Locke, and in the meanwhile he supposed that he ought to woo her, or court her, or do something of the kind. He was not in the least shy, but he had not the faintest idea how to woo a woman. The very notion of such a proceeding struck him as highly ridiculous and almost second-rate. It was like an old-fashioned notion.

"Esmé," he said, "what do people do before they propose? I suppose they lead up to it in some absurd way. If I were a rustic I could go and sit upon a stile with a straw in my mouth, and whistle at Lady Locke, while she stood staring at me and giggling. But I am not a rustic—I am an artist. Really, I don't see what I can do. Will she expect something?"

"My dear Reggie, women always expect something. Women are like minors, they live upon their expectations."

"Well, then," Reggie said petulantly, "what am I to do? Shall I ask her to take a walk, or what? I really can't put my arm round her waist. One owes something to oneself in spite of all the nonsense that Ibsen talks."

"One owes everything to oneself, and I also owe a great deal to other people—a great deal that I hope to live long enough never to repay. A debt of honour is one of the finest things in the world. The very name recalls a speech out of 'Guy Livingstone.' By the way, I sometimes wish that I had been born swart, as he was. I should have pleased Miss Rhoda Broughton, and she is so deliciously prosaic. Is she not the woman who said that she was always inspired to a pun by the sight of a cancer hospital? or am I thinking of Helen Mathers? I can never tell them apart—their lack of style is so marvellously similar. Why do women always write in the present tense, Reggie? Is it because they have no past? To go about without a past, must be like going about without one's trousers. I should feel positively indecent."

"There is no such thing as indecency, Esmé, just as there are no such things as right and wrong. There are only art and imbecility. But how shall I prepare for my proposal? What did you do?"

"I did nothing. My wife proposed to me, and I refused her. Then she went and put up some things called banns, I believe. Afterwards she sent me a white waistcoat in a brown paper parcel, and told me to meet her at a certain church on a certain day. I declined. She came in a hired carriage—a thing like a large deep bath, with two enormously fat parti-coloured horses—to fetch me. To avoid a scene I went with her, and I understand that we were married. But the colour of the window behind the altar was so atrocious, and the design—of Herodias carrying about the head of John the Baptist on a dish—so inartistically true to life, that I could not possibly attend to the service."

"Poor Esmé!" said Lord Reggie, in a tone charged with pathos. "I must trust in my intuitions, then."

"That is like trusting in one's convictions, Reggie. For the sake of the stars do not be sensible. I would far rather see you lying in your grave. Trust rather in your emotions."

"But I have none about Lady Locke. How could you suppose so?"

"I never suppose. I leave that to the heads of departments when they are answering questions in the House. It is the privilege of incompetence to suppose. The artist will always know. But there is Lady Locke, Reggie, being sensible in the rose garden. What must the roses think of her? Go to her, Reggie, tell her that you do not love her, and will marry her. That is what a true woman loves to hear."

As Lord Reggie went away, walking very delicately, with his head drooping towards his left shoulder, and his hands dangling in a dilettante manner at his sides, Madame Valtesi appeared at the French window of the drawing-room, refusing to join Tommy in some boyish game. After a parleying, which she conducted in profile, she turned her full face round, and having shaken her tormentor off, she proceeded slowly towards Amarinth, with an expression of extreme and illimitable irritability.

"Children are more lacking in discernment than the beasts of the field," she said, as she came up to him. "That boy is actually vexed because I will not go and play at Tom Tiddler's Ground with him. He positively expected that I would be Tiddler! Tiddler! Did you ever hear of such a name! It sounds like one of Dickens's characters. He says that all you have to do is to run about! Give me the long chair, please. He has almost succeeded in making me feel like Tiddler. It is a dreadful sensation."

She fanned herself slowly and looked round.

"Who is that in the rose garden?" she asked, putting up her eyeglass. "Oh! Lady Locke and Lord Reggie—an ill-assorted couple. They ought to marry."

"Why, dear lady?" said Esmé.

"Because they are ill-assorted. Affinities never marry nowadays. They always run away together and live on the Continent, waiting for decrees nisi. We repent of what we do so hastily nowadays. People divorce each other almost on sight. Will Lady Locke accept him?"

"Do widows ever refuse?"

"I am a widow."

"Indeed! I did not know it, or, if I ever knew it, I had forgotten. You are so delightfully married in your conduct."

"Was it Whistler who said that first?"

"No, I believe it comes originally from the Dutch. But it is my own adaptation, and I am too modest to put my name on a programme. Ah! Madame Valtesi, why have I never set the world in a blaze? I have plied the bellows most industriously, and I have made the twigs crackle, yet the fire splutters a good deal. Perhaps I have too much genius. Can it be that? My good things are in everybody's mouth."

"That's just it. You ought to have swallowed a cork years and years ago."

"Like Mr. Henry James. I always know when he has thought of a clever thing at a party."

"How?"

"By his leaving it immediately, and in total silence. He rushes home to write his thought down. His memory is treacherous."

"And does he often have to leave a party?"

"Pretty often. About once a year, I believe."

"It must be very trying socially to be so clever. So Lord Reggie is actually serious?"

"I hope he is never that. He will marry, as he sins, prettily, with the gaiety of a young Greek god."

"Marry and not settle down, as we all do now? We have improved upon the old code."

"We have practically abolished codes in London. In the country I fancy they continue to think of the commandments. How many commandments are there?"

"I forget! Seven, I think, or is it seventeen? Probably seventeen. I know there are a great many. I heard of a clergyman in a northern parish who took twenty minutes to read them, although he left out all the h's. Lady Locke and Lord Reggie have wandered away. It is like the garden scene of 'Faust.' Martha ought to come on now with Mephistopheles. Ah! here are Mrs. Windsor and tea. They will have to do instead."

Although Lord Reggie was such a novice in wooing, and would very much have preferred being wooed, he managed to convey to the mind of Lady Locke the notion that he had some vague intentions towards her. And that evening, as she dressed for dinner, she asked herself plainly what they were. That he loved her, she did not even for a moment imagine. She was not much given to self-deception. That he loved her money, a far more reasonable supposition as she mentally allowed—she did not really and honestly believe. For Lord Reggie, whatever were his faults, always conveyed the impression of being entirely thoughtless and improvident about worldly affairs. He had everything he wanted, naturally. Any other condition would have been wholly impossible to him, and would have seemed painfully out of place, and foreign to the scheme of the world, to those who knew him. But he never appeared to bother about any means for obtaining things, and Lady Locke thought him the last boy in the universe to lay a plot for the obtaining of a fortune. Had he, then, conceived a light passing fancy for her? She thought this possible, though a little unlikely. He was so different from the other men whom she had known, that she could never "place" him, or feel that she knew at all what his mind was likely to do under given conditions, or in cut and dried situations. Undoubtedly he had begun to think about her as well as about himself, an unusual conjunction, which no one would have anticipated. But exactly how he thought about her, Lady Locke could not tell; nor could she precisely tell either how she thought about him. He began to mean something to her. That was all she could say even to herself. She dressed for dinner very slowly that evening. Her window was open, and as she was pinning some yellow roses in the front of her gown, having dismissed her maid, she heard the piping, excited voice of Tommy asking a question of some hidden companion in the garden below.

"How does it get like that?" he exclaimed, with the penetrating squeak of a very young child. "I don't see. Does it grow?"

"No, Tommy," replied the soft voice of Lord Reggie, "nothing grows like that. It is too strange and beautiful to have grown."

"Well then, Reggie, do they paint it?"

"Never mind how it is done. That is the mistake we continually make. If the dolls dance exquisitely we should ignore the man who pulls the wires. Results are everything. When we see you in that pretty ivory-coloured suit we are content that you are pretty; we don't wish to learn how every button is buttoned, how every string is tied."

"There aren't any strings," cried Tommy. "Boys don't have strings."

"We don't care to find out how the tailor cuts and fashions, how he sews and stitches. He does all this in order that you may be beautiful. And we have only to think of you. Do you love this carnation, Tommy, as I love it? Do you worship its wonderful green? It is like some exquisite painted creature with dyed hair and brilliant eyes. It has the supreme merit of being perfectly unnatural. To be unnatural is often to be great. To be natural is generally to be stupid. To-morrow I will give you a carnation, Tommy, and you shall wear it at church when you go to hear my beautiful anthem."

Tommy gave vent to ecstatic cries of joy.

Lady Locke, standing by the window, reddened all over her face, and a fire flashed suddenly in her usually calm and gentle eyes. She threw the yellow roses roughly down upon her dressing-table and went hastily out of the room, leaving the door open behind her. When she reached the drawing-room she called her boy in from the garden.

"Tommy," she said, "it is past eight. Run away to bed. You were very late last night."

The child immediately began to protest; but she cut him short.

"Off with you," she cried. "Make haste. I can see you are looking tired."

"I am not tired, mother," said the boy, preparing to whimper.

"Tired or not, you must go when I say it," answered Lady Locke, with a harshness such as she had never displayed before. "Don't dispute about the matter, but go straight off. My boy must be like a soldier and obey the orders of his superior officer. I am your superior officer."

She pointed to the door, and Tommy departed reluctantly, with a very red face, and the menacing expression of an angry, governed child.

Lord Reggie came in from the garden. He found Lady Locke apparently immersed in the foreign intelligence of the *Times* Supplement.

.   .   .   .   .   .

That evening, after dinner, Lady Locke said to Lord Reggie—

"I don't want my little boy to wear flowers. He is too young. I heard you promising him a carnation for to-morrow. You mustn't think me rude, but, please, don't give him one."

Lord Reggie looked rather surprised.

"I am afraid he will be disappointed," he said.

"I cannot help that. And he will have forgotten it in five minutes. Children are as volatile as—as—"

"As lovers," said Madame Valtesi, who was smoking a cigarette in a chair by the window. "And forget as soon."

"Every one forgets," Esmé Amarinth said, with a gracious smile that illuminated his large features with slow completeness. "It is only when we have learned to love forgetfulness that we have learned the art of living. I wish people would forget me; but somehow they never do. Long after I have completely forgotten them they remember me. Then I have to pretend that I remember them, and that is so fatiguing."

"Esmé," said Mrs. Windsor, "do sing us your song of the passer-by. That is all about remembering and forgetting, and all that sort of thing. So sweet. I remember it made me cry when I heard it—or was it laugh? Which did you mean it to do?"

"I did not mean it to do anything. The poet who means much is little of a poet. I will sing you the song; but it is dreadfully direct in expression. I wrote it one night at Oxford when I was supremely drunk. I remember I wept as I wrote, great, wonderful tears. Yes, I will sing it. It is full of the sorrow, the white burnished sorrow of youth. How divine the melancholies of youth are! With age comes folly, and with folly comes the appalling merriment of experience. Experienced men are always merry. They see things as they really are. How terrible! until we can see things as they really are not we never truly live."

He went slowly to the piano, sat down, and played a plaintive, fleeting air—an air that was like a wandering moonbeam, the veritable phantom of a melody. Then he sang this song, in a low and almost toneless voice, uttering the notes rather than vocalising them.

THE SONG OF THE PASSER-BY.

Passing, passing—ah! sad heart, sing;
  But you cannot keep me beyond to-day,
For I am a wayward bird on the wing—
  A wayward waif, who will never stay.
The ivory morn, and the primrose eve,
  And the twilight, whispering late and low,
They kiss the hem of the spell I weave;
  They tremble, and ask me where I go.

Passing, passing—ah! sweet soul, sigh;
  But you cannot keep me beyond to-night,
For I am a wilful wanderer by—
  A wilful waif on a fanciful flight.
The shadowy moon, and the crimson star,
  And the wind that steals from the Western wave,
They watch the ways where my wild wings are;
  They murmur and marvel what I crave.

Passing, passing—ah! passion glow;
   But you cannot light me a lasting flame,
By which I may linger, linger and know
   My spark and yours from one furnace came.
You whisper and weep, and your words are tears,
   And your tears are words I remember yet;
But the flame dies down with the dying years,
   And nothing lives that forgets to forget.

Passing, passing—ah! whither? Why?
   Does the heart know why? Can the soul say where?
I pass, but I pause to catch ev'ry cry,
   To watch ev'ry face, be it foul or fair.
I must hear all the notes of the nightingales—
   Do they sing to a God or to graven things—
And not till the last faint flute-note fails
   Will I stay my flight, will I fold my wings.

When the last chord died away, Mrs. Windsor's voice was heard saying—

"I remember now, it made me cry. How dismal it is."

"Yes," said Madame Valtesi, "as dismal as a wet Derby or a day at the seaside. I hope your anthem will be more lively, Lord Reggie. But of course it will. We always keep our sorrows for the drawing-room, and our chirpiness for church. For sheer godless merriment commend me to the grand chant. It always reminds me of the conspirators' chorus in the 'Huguenots.' I used to hear it as a child. One hears so many things as a child, doesn't one? Childhood is one long career of innocent eavesdropping, of hearing what one ought not to hear."

"Yes," said Esmé, getting up from the piano. "And maturity is one long career of saying what one ought not to say. That is the art of conversation. Only one must always say it with intention, otherwise people think one grossly improper. Intention is everything. Artless impropriety is quite played out. Yvette Guilbert gave it its death-blow. It only lingers now in the writings of Ouida and the poems of Arthur Symons. Why are minor poets so artless, and why do they fancy they are so wicked? What curious fancies even unintelligent people have. No minor poet has ever been wicked, just as no real artist has ever been good. If one intends to be good, one must take it up as a profession. It is quite the most engrossing one in the world. Have you ever been with a good person who is taking a holiday from being good? It is like falling into the Maelstrom. They carry you off your feet. Their enjoyment terrifies the imagination. They are like a Sunday school let loose in the Moulin Rouge, or Mr. Toole when he has made a pun! Sometimes I wish that I could be good too, in order to have such a holiday. Are you really going to bed, Lady Locke? Eleven! I had no idea it was so early. I am going to sit up all night with Reggie, saying mad scarlet things, such as George Meredith loves, and waking the night with silver silences. Good-night. Come, Reggie, let us go to the smoking-room, since we are left alone. I will be brilliant for you as I have never been brilliant for my publishers. I will talk to you as no character in my plays has ever talked. Come! The young Endymion stirs in his dreams, and the pale-souled Selene watches him from her pearly car. The shadows on the lawns are violet, and the stars wash the spaces of the sky with primrose and with crimson. The night is old yet. Let me be brilliant, dear boy, or I feel that I shall weep for sheer wittiness, and die, as so many have died, with all my epigrams still in me."

XII

THE cottage was full of the curious suppressed rustling that seems to be inseparable from church-going in England. Good people invariably rustle, and so bad people, trying to be good, are inclined to rustle too. At least that was what Madame Valtesi said as she stood in the tiny, sage-green hall hung with fans, and finished buttoning her long Suède gloves. She still wore her big and shady hat. She declared it made her feel religious, and nobody was prepared to dispute the assertion. Tommy was clamouring for his promised green carnation; but Lord Reggie, in obedience to Lady Locke's request, told him that the one he had intended for him had faded away in the night, had faded exquisitely, as the wicked fade after flourishing like green bay trees; and Tommy, though inclined to tears, was soothed by a promise that he should sit on the organ seat and turn over in the anthem. Lady Locke looked rather serious, and Mrs. Windsor strangely dissipated. She always did look particularly dissipated on Sunday mornings, although she was not aware of it; and to-day she was intent on being decisively rustic, and as countrified in her piety as possible. She wore an innocent gown powdered with pimpernels, and a little bonnet that she thought holiness itself, consisting as it did of a very small bow and a very large spike. Lord Reggie and Esmé Amarinth honoured the day with frock coats and tall hats; and the former was in a state of considerable excitement about his anthem.

Through the drowsy summer air the five bells of Chenecote Church chimed delicately, and prayer-books were at a premium. Everybody except Lady Locke had come down without one, and Mrs. Windsor was in despair.

"We must have them," she said piteously, "or the congregation will be dreadfully shocked. Congregations are so easily shocked in the country. I wonder if the servants have any? Servants always have prayer-books and that kind of thing, don't they? I will ask."

She rang the bell and one of the tall footmen appeared.

"Simpson, we want four prayer-books," she said. "Are there any in the house?"

Simpson looked exceedingly doubtful, but said he would go and see. Eventually he returned with three.

"There is one more, ma'am—the upper housemaid's," he said, handing them on a salver. "But she wrote comments in it when she belonged to the Salvation Army, and she can't rub them out, ma'am, so she don't like to show it."

"Really!" said Mrs. Windsor, looking mystified. "Well, never mind, we must try and manage with these. Oh! Lord Reggie, you won't want one, of course, because you will be behind the curtain. I forgot that. We are going to walk. It is only ten minutes or so, and I thought it would be more rustic, especially as the roads are dusty. Now, I think we ought to start. If we are late it will create a scandal, and Mr. Smith will be horrified."

"How dutiful the atmosphere is!" Madame Valtesi said to Amarinth as they set forth. "We are so frightfully punctual that I feel quite like an early Christian. I wonder why the Christians were always so early before we were born? They are generally very late now."

"I suppose they have grown tired," he answered, arranging the carnation in his button-hole meditatively. "Probably we suffer from the activity of our forefathers. When I feel fatigued I always think that my grandfather must have been what is called an excellent walker. How very Sabbath the morning is!"

There was, in fact, a Sunday air in the quiet country road. The geese had ceased from their mundane proceedings in the pond, and were meditating over their sins in some cloistered nook of the farm-yard. The fields looked greenly pious, emptied as they were of labourers. In the flowery hedgerows the birds chirped with a chastened note; and even the summer wind touched the walkers as a bishop touches the heads of kneeling candidates at Confirmation. Or so, at least, Lady Locke thought, with a pleasant fancifulness that she kept entirely to herself. The bells chimed on monotonously; and now and then, as they walked, they caught sight of neatly-dressed rustics in front of them, strolling mildly to the church, tricked out in all the black bravery of broadcloth, or decked in sprigged muslins and chip hats.

Mrs. Windsor was quite delighted.

"Is not this novel?" she exclaimed, setting her white veil straight, and spreading a huge parasol to the sun. "I feel so righteous. It is pleasant to feel righteous, isn't it? So much pleasanter than to be good. I hope Mr. Smith will not preach a long sermon; but he looks rather like a man who would. People who have nothing to say always do preach long sermons, don't they? They keep hoping they will have something to say presently, I suppose?"

"And they hope out loud," said Madame Valtesi. "People who hope out loud are very trying. I know so many. Dear me, how dusty it is! I feel as if I were drowning. Are we nearly there?"

"Yes," said Mrs. Windsor; "there is the common—that is the common where Mr. Smith has checked the rowdyism. I wish he had not broken up all the idle corners before we came. I should so like to have met one."

"Mr. Smith has decidedly been premature," Amarinth said gravely. "Clergymen often are. They take away our sins before we have had time to sit down with them. There go the school children, I suppose. They look intensely clean. So many people look intensely clean, and nothing else. That is all one can say about them. Half the men I know have absolutely no other characteristic. Their only talent is that they know how to wash. Perhaps that is why men of genius so seldom wash. They are afraid of being mistaken for men of talent. What will happen when we come into church? Will everybody stand up?"

"I hope you will all sit down to hear my anthem," Lord Reggie said, rather nervously. "It will be much better. Please, do! Lady Locke, will you promise to sit down? People attend so much more closely when they are sitting. If they stand up they always look about and think all the time about sitting down."

"Just as when people are asking you to stay they are always wondering if you will go," said Madame Valtesi, casting a vicious glance at Tommy, who was delightedly stirring up the dust.

"I will sit down certainly," said Lady Locke, "if you wish it; but I could listen equally well standing. I do hope Jimmy Sands will sing his little bit of solo correctly; I shall feel quite nervous till it is over."

Lord Reggie looked at her with earnest pleasure, and even with a momentary affection. He had never liked her so much before.

"Don't any of you stare at him while he is singing," he said, "or he will get sharp. He always does; I have noticed it."

"What a pity staring does not have that effect upon all of us," said Madame Valtesi. "London would be quite brilliant. I have looked at people for hours, but they have never got sharp."

"There goes the five minutes' bell," said Lady Locke; "we are just in time."

When they reached the churchyard Lord Reggie and Tommy went round to the vestry, and the rest of the party made their way to a front pew, amid the suppressed excitement of the rest of the congregation. Mr. Amarinth especially created a sensation; but he always expected to do that. Ever since he had made a name for himself by declaring that he was pleased with the Equator, and desired its further acquaintance, he had been talked about. Whenever the public interest in him showed signs of flagging he wrote an improper story, or published an epigram in one volume, on handmade paper, with immense margins, or produced a play full of other people's wit, or said something scandalous about the North Pole. He had ruined the reputation of more than one eminently respectable ocean which had previously been received everywhere, and had covered Nature with confusion by his open attacks upon her. Just now he was living upon his green carnation, which had been freely paragraphed in all the papers; and when that went out of vogue he had some intention of producing a revised version of the Bible, with all the inartistic passages cut out, and a rhymed dedication to Mr. Stead, whose *Review of Reviews* always struck him as only a degree less comic than the books of that arch-humourist Miss Edna Lyall, or the bedroom imaginings of Miss Olive Schreiner. The villagers of Chenecote gaped open-mouthed at his green carnation and crimped hair; and the exhortation, as delivered in a *presto* mumble by Mr. Smith, was received with general apathy, as the opera of "Faust" is received on an off night in the opera season.

Lord Reggie and Tommy were completely hidden behind the curtain that shielded the organ seat; but the presence and agitation of the former were indicated by the confused perambulations of Jimmy Sands, who was perpetually dodging to and fro in a flushed manner between his place and the organ, receiving instructions, and conveying whispered directions to his youthful colleagues in the choir. The village organist had been deposed from his high estate for the time being, and Lord Reggie commanded the organ entirely— this fact becoming apparent during the service in the abrupt alternations of loud and soft, the general absence of pedal notes, and the continued employment of the *vox humana* as a solo stop during the singing of the psalms, to the undoing of the men in the choir, and the extreme astonishment of the unused congregation. At the beginning of the second lesson, too, Lord Reggie made his presence known by the performance of a tumultuous and unexpected obligato, which completely drowned the opening verses of the fourth chapter of the Gospel according to St. Matthew, and caused the painted windows at the extreme end of the church to crackle in a manner that suggested earthquakes and the last great day.

"What is he doing?" whispered Madame Valtesi to Amarinth. "Is it in the thirty-nine articles?"

"No," replied Esmé; "he is only getting up from his seat. How wonderful he is! I never heard anything more impressive in my life. After all, unpremeditated art is the greatest art. Such an effect as that could never have been produced except impromptu."

The anthem passed off fairly well, although Jimmy Sands went rather flat, perhaps owing to the fact that none of the party from the cottage so much as glanced at him during his performance.

"He evidently made allowance for our staring," Madame Valtesi said afterwards. "However, it can't be helped; we shall know better another time. I thought his singing flat gave a touch of real character to the anthem."

Mrs. Windsor was congratulating Mr. Smith on his charming little service, and condoling with him on having been unable to pronounce the blessing. This formality had been rendered impossible by the ingenious action of Lord Reggie, who had forgotten about it, and evoked continuous music from the organ ever since the amen of the prayer preceding it, finally bursting into a loud fugue by Bach, played without the pedal part, just when the curate was venturing to meekly insert it into a second's interstice of comparative silence, brought about by the solo employment of the *vox humana* without accompaniment.

"However," said Mrs. Windsor, "I daresay it won't much matter for once in a way, will it? It is no good making ourselves miserable about comparative trifles."

"He might leave out a curse or two when he next reads the Commination Service, and balance matters in that way," said Madame Valtesi, aside to Amarinth.

"The rusticity of the service was quite delicious," Mrs. Windsor went on graciously. "So appropriate! Everything was so well chosen and in character! Ah, Mr. Smith, although you are a clergyman, I am certain you must have the artistic temperament."

"I trust not," Mr. Smith said very gravely—"I earnestly trust not. The artistic temperament is a sin that should be sternly struggled against, and, if possible, eliminated. In these modern days I notice that every wickedness that is committed is excused on the ground of temperament."

They were walking home across the common as he said this, and Lady Locke turned to Lord Reggie, who was by her side, still rather flushed by his exertions.

"Are you one of those who make a god of their temperament?" she said. "What Mr. Smith says seems to me rather true."

"I think one's temperament should be one's leader in life, certainly," he answered.

"The blind leading the blind."

"It is beautiful to be blind. Those who can see are always avoiding just the very things that would give them most pleasure. Esmé says that to know how to be led is a much greater art than to know how to lead."

"I don't care to hear the opinions of Mr. Amarinth," she answered, in a low voice. "His epigrams are his opinions. His actions are performed vicariously in conversation. If he were to be silent he would cease to live."

"You don't know Esmé at all, really," Reggie said.

"And you know him far too well," she answered.

He looked at her for a moment rather curiously.

XIII

UNDAY afternoon is always a characteristic time. Even irreligious people, who have no principles to send them to sleep, or to cause them to take a weekly walk, or to induce them to write an unnecessary letter to New Zealand—why are unnecessary letters to New Zealand invariably written on Sunday afternoons?—even irreligious people are generally in an unusual frame of mind on the afternoon of the day of rest. They don't feel week-day. There is a certain atmosphere of orthodoxy which affects them. Possibly it causes them to feel peculiarly unorthodox. Still, it affects them. In the country, in summer especially, Sunday afternoon lays a certain spell upon everybody. It goes to their heads. They fall under its strange influence, even against their will, and become, in a measure, different from themselves. Solemn people are often unnaturally flippant on Sunday afternoon, and flippant people frequently retire to bed on the verge of tears. The hearty bow-wow girl is conscious of being unpleasantly chastened by some invisible power; and the stupid young man sinks into a strange apoplectic condition, with his chin sunk on his waistcoat, and his mind drowned in the waters of forgetfulness. Sloth is in the air, and a decorous desultoriness pervades humanity. It is as if thunder was in the social atmosphere. The repose is not quite natural. Those who are in high positions, and therefore have something to live down to, long to imitate the hapless rustic, and wander forth among the fields, sucking a straw, and putting their arm round a waist. Unmelodious persons are almost throttled by a desire to whistle; but the true singer feels as dumb as a tree. Lunch pervades the human consciousness, and the prospect of tea engages the mind to an extent which is neither quite normal nor entirely free from a suspicion of greediness. Dogs snore much louder than usual, and the confirmed sufferer from insomnia sleeps with an indecent soundness never attained by the beauty in the fairy tale. Undoubtedly, Sunday throws the world entirely out of gear, and that is one of its chief worldly charms. It is well to be out of gear at least once in the week.

This particular Sunday afternoon had not left the party at the cottage unscathed, as the acute observer would have immediately seen on penetrating into the pretty shady garden, with its formal rose walks, and its delightful misshapen yew trees. Madame Valtesi, for instance, was knitting, a thing she had scarcely ever been noticed to do within the memory of man. Mrs. Windsor was going about in garden gloves, with a spud and a pair of clippers, damaging the flower-beds, with an air of duty and almost sacred responsibility. Mr. Amarinth was reading the newspaper like a married man; and Lord Reggie was lying in a hammock, trying to kill flies by clapping his hands together. Lady Locke was indoors, writing the unnecessary letter to New Zealand, which has already been referred to; and Tommy, fatigued to tears by luncheon, had gone to bed, and was dreaming in an angry manner about black beetles, unable quite to attain the dignity of a nightmare, and yet deprived of the sweet repose which is popularly believed to shut the door on the nose of the doctor.

Yes, decidedly, it was Sunday afternoon!

The weather was very hot and languid, and the bees kept on buzzing all the time. Bung was engaged in investigating the coal-hole, apparently under the impression that hidden treasure was not foreign to its soil; and conversation entirely languished. Madame Valtesi dropped her stitches, Lord Reggie failed to kill his flies, and Mr. Amarinth misunderstood the drift of leading articles. The Sabbath mind was very much in evidence, and the Sabbath mind verges on imbecility. The bells chiming for afternoon service rose on the still air, and died away; but nobody moved. Evidently enthusiasm for rusticity combined with religion was fading away. A silence reigned, and the hour for tea drew slowly on. But presently Amarinth, after reading all the advertisements on the cover of his newspaper, put it down slowly and glanced around, with the puffy expression of a person suppressing a grown-up yawn.

His eyes wandered about, to Mrs. Windsor immersed in amateur gardening of the destructive kind, to Lord Reggie in his hammock, to Madame Valtesi dropping stitches in her low chair. He sighed and spoke—

"Newspapers are very enervating," he said. "I wonder what a journalist is like? I always imagine him a person with a very large head—with the particular sort of large head, you know, that is large because it contains absolutely nothing."

"I thought journalists were the people who sell newspapers at the street corners," said Lord Reggie.

"Oh! I don't fancy they are so picturesque as that," said Esmé, again suppressing a yawn. "Madame Valtesi, you ought to know; you run a theatre, and people who run theatres always know journalists. It seems to be in the blood."

"How can I talk?" she replied. "Don't you see that I am knitting?"

"Are you doing a stitch in time, the sort of stitch that is supposed to rhyme with nine? I wonder why it is that we always give ourselves up to occupations that we dislike on Sunday. I have not read a newspaper for years. One learns so much more about what is happening in the world if one never opens a newspaper. I once wrote an article for a newspaper, but that was before I had met Sala. Ever since then I have been haunted by the fear that if I did it again I might grow like him. I believe he has lived in Mexico. His style always strikes me as decidedly Mexican. I met him at dinner, and he told me facts that I did not previously know, all the time I was trying to eat. Afterwards in the drawing-room he gave a lecture. I rather forget the subject, but I think it was, 'Eggs I have known.' He knew a great many. It was very instructive and uninteresting. I think he said he had patented it. How does one patent a lecture?"

"Esmé, you are talking nonsense!" Madame Valtesi said, dropping two more stitches with an air of purpose.

"I hope I am. People who talk sense are like people who break stones in the road: they cover one with dust and splinters. What is Mrs. Windsor doing?"

"Looking for slugs," said Lord Reggie.

"Why?"

"To kill them."

"How dreadful! They live such gentle lives among the roses. Do let us talk about religion. I want to try and feel appropriate. Ah! here is Lady Locke. Lady Locke, we were just going to begin talking about religion."

"Indeed!" she said, coming forward slowly, and looking a little colonial after the completion of her task. "Do you know anything about the subject?"

"No. That is why I want to talk about it. Vivacious ignorance is so artistic."

"It is too common to be that," said Madame Valtesi. "Ignorant people are always vivacious, just as really clever men never wear spectacles. Wearing spectacles is the most played-out pose I know. I wonder the Germans still keep it up."

"A nation that keeps up their army would keep up anything," said Esmé. "Germans always talk about foreign politics and native beer. Oh! Mrs. Windsor has just permitted a slug to live. I can see that by the way in which she is taking off her gloves and trying not to look magnanimous. Is it nearly tea-time, Mrs. Windsor?" he added, as she came up, a little flushed with under exertion. "I only ask because I am not thirsty. Tea is one of those delightful things that one takes because one does not want it. That is why we are all so passionately fond of it. It is like death, exquisitely unnecessary."

"I have found several slugs," she answered triumphantly, "but I can't kill them. They move so fast, at least when they are frightened. You would never believe it. I came upon one under a leaf just now, and it started just like a person disturbed in a nap. It fell right off the leaf, and I couldn't find it again."

"I suppose slugs have nerves, then," Reggie said, getting up out of his hammock, "and get strung up like people who over-work. Just think of a strung-up slug! There is something weird in the idea. A slug that started at its own shadow. Here is tea! Oh, Mrs. Windsor, where are the tents to be for the school treat to-morrow?"

"At the end of the croquet lawn. Mr. Smith says the children are terribly excited about it. Esmé, you must address the children before they sing their hymn on going away. They always end with a hymn. Mr. Smith thinks it quiets them."

"I wonder if singing a hymn would quiet me when I am excited," said Esmé, musing over his tea-cup.

"Are you ever excited?" asked Lady Locke.

"Sometimes, when I have invented a perfect paradox. A perfect paradox is so terribly great. It makes one feel like a trustee. Can you understand the sensation? Have you ever felt like a trustee?"

"I don't think I have," Lady Locke said, laughing.

"Then, dear lady, you have never yet really lived. To-morrow I shall feel like a trustee, for I am going to invent some marvellous pale paradoxes for the children—paradoxes like early dew-drops with the sun upon them. Mrs. Windsor, I shall address the children upon the art of folly, upon the wonderful art of being foolish beautifully. After they are tired with their games and their graceful Arcadian frolics, gather them in an irregular group under that cedar tree, and while the absurd sun goes down, endeavouring, as the sun nearly always does in country places, to imitate Turner's later pictures, I will speak to them wonderful words of strange and delicate meaning, words that they can easily forget. The only things worth saying are those that we forget, just as the only things worth doing are those that the world is surprised at!"

"The world is surprised at nearly everything," said Lord Reggie. "It was surprised when Miss Margot Tennant married only a Home Secretary! A world that could be surprised at that could be surprised at anything. The world is surprised at Esmé because he does not know how to make a pun, and because he dares to show the French what can be done with their drama. The world is surprised at me because I never go to Hurlingham, and because I have never read Mrs. Humphry Ward's treatises! The world is even surprised when Mr. Gladstone is found to have been born in several places at the same time—as if he would be born at different times! —and when M. Zola turns out to be crazily respectable. When is the world not surprised?"

"Virtue in any form astonishes the world," Madame Valtesi said. "I once did a good action. When I was very young I married the only man who did not love me. I thought he ought to be converted. Every one who knew me was astounded."

"If the world is surprised at good actions," Lady Locke said, "it is our own fault. We have trained it."

"Nothing is more painful to me than to come across virtue in a person in whom I have never previously suspected its existence," said Esmé, putting down his tea-cup with a graceful gesture of abnegation. "It is like finding a needle in a bundle of hay. It pricks you. If we have virtue we should warn people of it. I once knew a woman who fell down dead because she found a live mouse in the pocket of her gown. A live virtue is a like a live mouse. Indeed, the surprises of virtue are far greater than the surprises of vice. We are never surprised when we hear that a man has gone to the bad; but who can fathom our wonderment when we are obliged to believe that he has gone to the good?"

"I hate a good man," Madame Valtesi said, with a certain dignity.

"Then you ought to lead one about with you in a string," said Esmé. "It is so splendid to have some one always near to hate. It is like spending the day with a hurricane, or being born an orphan. I once knew a man who had been born an orphan. He had been so fortunate as never to have experienced the tender care of a mother, or the fostering anxiety of a father. There was something great about him, the greatness of a man who has never known trouble. Why are we not all born orphans?"

"I dare say it is a pity," Mrs. Windsor said rather sleepily. "It would save our parents a lot of trouble."

"And our children a great deal of anxiety," said Esmé. "I have two boys, and their uneasiness about my past is as keen as my uneasiness about their future. I am afraid they will be good boys. They are fond of cricket, and loathe reading poetry. That is what Englishmen consider goodness in boys."

"And what do they consider goodness in girls?" asked Lady Locke.

"Oh, girls are always good till they are married," said Madame Valtesi. "And after that it isn't supposed to matter."

"English girls are like country butter," said Esmé—"fresh. That is all one can say about them."

"And that is saying a good deal," said Lady Locke.

"I don't think so," said Lord Reggie. "Nothing is really worth much till it is a trifle stale. A soul that is fresh is hardly a soul at all. Sensations give the grain to the wood, the depth and dignity to the picture. No fruit is so worthless as the fruit with the bloom upon it."

"Yes," said Esmé. "The face must be young, but the soul must be old. The face must know nothing, the soul everything. Then fascination is born."

"Perhaps merely an evil fascination," said Lady Locke.

"Fascination is art. I recognise no good or evil in art," Esmé answered. "In England we have no art, just because we do recognise good and evil. Glasgow thinks it is shameful to be naked; yet even the Bible declares that the ideal condition is to be naked and unashamed; and Glasgow, being in Scotland, naturally gives the lead to England. We have no art. We have only the Royal Academy, which is remarkable merely for the badness of its cuisine, and the coiffure of its well-meaning President. Our artists, as they call themselves, are like Mr. Grant Allen: they say that all their failures are 'pot-boilers.' They love that word. It covers so many sins of commission. They set down their incompetence as an assumption, which makes it almost graceful, and stick up the struggle for life as a Moloch requiring the sacrifice of genius. And then people believe in the travesty. Mr. Grant Allen could have been Darwin, no doubt; but Darwin could never have been Mr. Grant Allen. But what is the good of trying to talk about what does not exist. There is no such thing as art in England."

"Shall we talk of the last new novel?" said Madame Valtesi. "Unfortunately I have not read it. I am told it is full of improper epigrams, and has not the vestige of a plot. So like life!"

"Some one said to me the other day that life was like a French farce," said Mrs. Windsor—"so full of surprises."

"Not the surprises of a French farce, I hope," said Madame Valtesi. "Esmé, I am quite stiff from knitting so long. Take me to the drawing-room and sing to me a song of France. Let us try to forget England."

"Lady Locke, will you come for a stroll in the yew tree walk?" said Reggie. "I see Mrs. Windsor is trying to read 'Monsieur, Madame, et Bébé'! She always reads that on Sunday!"

Lady Locke assented.

XIV

HEN Lord Reggie asked Lady Locke to come with him into the yew tree walk that Sunday afternoon, he fully intended to tell her that he would be glad to marry her. It seemed to him that Sunday was a very appropriate day for such a confession, and would give to his remarks a solemnity that they might otherwise lack. But somehow the conversation became immediately unmanageable, as conversations have a knack of doing, and turned into channels which had less than nothing to do with marriage. By a series of ingenious modulations Lord Reggie might doubtless have contrived eventually to arrive at the key in which he wanted to breathe out his love song; but the afternoon was too sultry for ingenuities, and so they talked about the influence of Art on Nature, and his anthem, until it was time to dress for dinner.

Lady Locke was a woman, and so it may be taken for granted that she divined her companion's original intention, and was perhaps a little amused at his failure to carry it into an act. But she manifested no consciousness, and disappeared to her bedroom without displaying either disappointment or triumph. She did, however, in fact know that Lord Reggie meant to ask her the fateful question, and she had quite decided now how she meant to answer it.

She had fallen into a curious sort of fondness for this tired, unnatural boy, whom she considered as twisted as if he had been an Egyptian cripple, zigzagging along a sandy track on his hands with his legs tied round his neck; and two or three days ago she had even thought seriously what she would say to him if he asked her to join lives with him permanently. The motherly feeling had verged on something else, very different; and when one day he carelessly touched her hand she had felt her heart beating with a violence that was painfully natural. But now, more than one incident that had since occurred had forged links in a new chain of resolution that held her back from a folly. Although possibly she hardly knew it, the scrap of conversation that she had chanced to overhear between Lord

Reggie and Tommy had really decided her to meet the former with a refusal if he asked her to be his wife. It had opened her eyes, and shown her in a flash the influence that a mere pose may have upon others who are not posing. Her mother's heart flushed with a heat of anger at the idea of Tommy, her dead soldier's son, developing into the sort of young man whom she chose to christen " Modern " ; and as her heart flushed, unknown to her her mind really decided. She still fancied that Lord Reggie was nothing more than a whimsical *poseur*, bitten by the tarantula of imitation that preys upon weak natures. She still fancied what she hoped. But incertitude strengthened resolve, and she never intended to be Lady Reggie Hastings. Yet she meant Lord Reggie to propose to her. She liked him so well that, womanlike, she could not quite forbear the pleasure of hearing him even pretend that he loved her—she supposed he would feel bound to pretend so much; and his proposal would give to her an opportunity of saying one or two things to him—of preaching that affectionate sermon, in fact, that she had long ago written in her thoughts.

Sweet women love to preach to those whom they like, and Lady Locke liked Lord Reggie very much, and wished strongly to have the chance of telling him so.

But he said nothing that night, and she had to wait for a while. The weather, which had certainly shown the most graceful politeness to the Surrey week, was still in a complaisant frame of mind when Monday morning dawned, and the tents were put up for the school children, and the Aunt Sallies and other instruments of amusement were posed in their places about the garden, without any fear arising lest the rain should prevent their being used. Esmé Amarinth spent the morning in reflecting upon his address, and constructing pale paradoxes; and the rest of the party at the "Retreat" did nothing, with all the quiet ingenuity that seems inbred in the English race.

At four o'clock the sound of lusty singing in the dusty distance announced the approach of the expected guests, who, under the direction of Mr. Smith, expressed their youthful feelings of anticipation and excitement in a processional hymn, whose words dealt with certain ritualistic doctrines in a spirit of serene but rather incompetent piety, and whose tune was remarkable for the Gounod spirit that pervaded its rather love-lorn harmonies. As Mr. Amarinth said, it sounded like a French apostrophe to a Parisian

Eros, and was tinged with the amorous music colour of Covent
Garden.

Mrs. Windsor received the party with weary grace, and a general
salute that might have included all the national schools in the king-
dom, so wide and so impersonal was its manner. She impressed the
children as much as Madame Valtesi frightened them by examining
them with a stony and sphinx-like gravity through her tortoiseshell
eye-glass. The teachers conducted the programme of games—in
which, however, Lady Locke, Tommy, and Lord Reggie fitfully
took part; and after tea had been munched with trembling delight
in the largest of the tents, and more games had been got through,
Mr. Smith distributed small presents to all the children, some of
whom were quite unstrung by the effort they had to make not to
seem too happy in the presence of "the quality." The curate
then took his leave, as he was obliged to visit a sick parishioner, and,
as the sun was evidently on the point of beginning to imitate
Turner's later pictures, Mrs. Windsor directed that the children
should be assembled under the great cedar tree on the lawn, to hear
Esmé Amarinth's promised address.

The picture that the garden presented at this moment was quite
a pretty one. The sun, as I have said, was declining towards the west
in a manner strongly suggestive of a scene at the Lyceum Theatre
after many rehearsals with a competent lime-light man. The monstrous yew trees cast gross misshapen shadows across the smooth,
velvet lawns. The air was heavy with the scents of flowers. Across
the gleaming yellow of the sky a black riband of homeward passing
rooks streamed slowly towards the trees they loved. Under the
spreading branches of the cedar stood the big motley group of flushed
and receptive children, flanked by their more staid teachers, and
faced by Bung, who sat upon his tail before them, and panted
serenely, with his tongue hanging out sideways nearly to the ground.
Dotted about upon creaking garden chairs were Mrs. Windsor,
Madame Valtesi, Lady Locke, and Lord Reggie, while Tommy in
a loose white sailor suit scampered about from one place to another,
simmering in perfect enjoyment. And the central figure of all was
Esmé Amarinth, who stood leaning upon an ebony stick with a silver
knob, surveying his audience with the peculiar smile of humorous
self-satisfaction that was so characteristic of his large-featured face.

Just before he began his address Mrs. Windsor fluttered up to him,
and whispered in his ear—

"Don't make any classical allusions, will you, Esmé? I promised Mr. Smith there should be nothing of that kind. He thinks classical allusions corrupting. Of course he's wrong—good people always are —but perhaps we ought to humour him, as he is the curate, you know."

Esmé assented with a graceful bend of his crimpled head, and in a clear and deliberate voice began to speak.

"The art of folly," he said, "that is to say, the art of being consciously foolish beautifully, has been practised to some extent in all ages, and among all peoples, from the pale, clear dawn of creation, when, as we are told, the man Adam, in glorious nudity, walked perfectly among the perfect glades of Eden, down to the golden noontide of this nineteenth century, in which we subtly live and subtly suffer. Always throughout the circling ages the soul of man has to some slight extent aspired after folly, as Nature aspires after Art, and as the old and learned aspire after the wonderful ignorance that lies hidden between the scarlet covers of the passionate book of youth. Always there have been in the world earnest men and earnest women striving with a sacred wisdom to compass the highest forms of folly, seeking with a manifold persistence to sound the depths of that violet main in which the souls of the elect rock to and fro eternally. But although, even in the morning of the world, there were earnest seekers after lies, the pursuit of ignorance has never been carried on with such unswerving fidelity and with so much lovely unreason as is the case to-day. We are beginning, only beginning, to understand some of the canons of the beautiful art of folly."

Here Esmé changed his ebony stick into his other hand, and glanced round at Lord Reggie, with a delicate smile of self-approbation. Then he proceeded, without clearing his throat.

"The mind of man has, however, always clung with a poetic persistence to certain fallacies which have greatly interfered with the proper progress of folly, and have terribly hindered the evolution of disorder out of order, and of unreason out of reason. To give only a few instances. For centuries upon centuries we have been told by those unenlightened beings called philosophers, sages, and thinkers, that children should obey their parents, that the old should direct the young, that Nature is the mother of beauty, and that wisdom is the parent of true greatness. For centuries upon centuries we have had instilled into us the malign conception that in renunciation we shall find peace, and in starvation the most satisfying plenty. Men and women have lived to be dumb, instead of living to speak; have stopped their ears to the alluring cries of folly; have gone to the grave with all their sublime absurdities still in them, unuttered, unexpressed, unimpressed upon the wildly sensible people by whom they have been surrounded and environed. The art of folly has been trampled in the dust by the majority; while poor reasonable human beings have been offering up sacrifices to propriety, respectability, common sense, and a thousand grotesque idols, whose very names fall as unmelodiously upon the ear as the shrill and monotonous discords of the nightingales that torture us with their murmurings towards the latter end of May—whose very names, when written down upon smooth paper, or, as formerly, graved upon tablets of wax with instruments of ivory, are as disagreeable to the eye as the crude colouring of the Atlantic Ocean, or the unimaginable ugliness of a fine summer's day in the midland counties of England. But at last there seems to be a prospect of better things, the flush of a wonderful dawn in the hitherto shadowy sky. A star with a crimson mouth has arisen in the East to guide wise men and women out of the strait and narrow way down which they have been stumbling so long. I believe, I tremblingly dare to believe, that a bright era of undisciplined folly is about to dawn over the modern world, and therefore I speak to you, beautiful pink children, and I ask you to recognise your youth, and your exquisite potentiality for foolishness. For in youth, only in delicate, delicious youth, can we acquire the rudiments of the beautiful art of folly. When we are old we are so crusted with the hideous lichen of wisdom and experience, so gnarled with thought, and weather-beaten with knowledge, that we can only teach. We have lost the power to learn, as all teachers infallibly do."

At this point in Esmé's address the face of the national school-master, a grey person, rather conceited in his own wisdom than wise in his own conceit, began to present—as a magic lantern presents pictures upon a sheet—various expressions, all of which partook of uneasiness and indignation. He glanced furtively around, stared defiantly at the children, and shifted from one foot to the other like a boy who is being lectured. Esmé observed his disquietude with considerable satisfaction.

"People teach in order to conceal their ignorance, as people smile in order to conceal their tears, or sin, too often, merely to draw away a curious observation from the amplitude and endurance of their virtue. The beautiful falling generation are learning to do things for their own sake, and not for the sake of Mrs. Grundy, who will soon sit alone in her dowdy disorder, a chaperon bereft of her débutante, the hopeless and frowsy leader of a lost and discredited cause. Yes, wisdom has nearly had its day, and the stars are beginning to twinkle in the violet skies of folly.

"It is not, alas! given to all of us to be properly foolish. The custom of succeeding ages has rendered wisdom a hereditary habit with thousands upon thousands of us, and even the destructive influence of myself, of Lord Reginald"—here he indicated Reggie, with one plump, white hand—"and of a few, a very few others, among whom I can include Mr. Oscar Wilde, has so far failed to uproot that pestilent plant from its home in the retentive soil of humanity. What was bad enough for our ridiculous fathers is still bad enough for too many of us. We are still content with the old virtues, and still timorous of the new vices. We still fear to clasp the radiant hands of folly, and drown our good impulses in the depths of her enchanted eyes. But many of us are comparatively elderly, and, believe me, the elderly quickly lose the divine power of faculty of disobedience. If it were my first word to you, children, I would say to you—learn to disobey. To know how to be disobedient is to know how to live."

The national schoolmaster at this point planted his feet in the first position with sudden violence, and gave vent to a hem that was a revelation of keen though inarticulate emotion. Esmé indicated that he had heard the sound by slightly elevating his voice.

"Learn," he said, "to disobey the cold dictates of reason; for reason acts upon life as the breath of frost acts upon water, and binds the leaping streams of the abnormal in the congealing and icy band of the normal. All that is normal is to be sedulously avoided. That is what the modern pupil will teach in the future his old-fashioned masters. That is what you may, if you will have the courage, impress upon the pastors and masters, who must learn to look to you for guidance."

Extreme disorder of mind was now made manifest in the fantastic postures assumed by the entire staff of teachers, who began to turn their feet in, to construct strange patterns with their fingers, and in all other known ways to mutely express the dire forebodings of those who feel that their empire is passing away from them.

"It has hitherto been the privilege of age to rule the world. In the blessed era of folly that privilege will be transferred to youth. Never forget, therefore, to be young, to be young, and, if possible, consciously foolish."

The expressions of the children at this point indicated intelligent acquiescence, and Esmé's face was irradiated with a tranquil smile.

"It is very difficult to be young, especially up to the age of thirty," he continued, "and very difficult to be properly foolish up to any age at all; but we must not despair. Genius is the art of not taking pains, and genius is more common than is generally supposed. If we do not take proper pains, there is no reason why even the cleverest among us should not in time learn to practise beautifully the beautiful art of folly. It is always well to be personal, and as egoism is scarcely less artistic than its own brother, vanity, I shall make no apology for now alluding, in as marked a manner as possible, to myself. I"—he spoke here with superb emphasis—"I am absurd. For years I have tried in vain not to hide it. For years I have striven to call public attention to my exquisite gift, to impress its existence upon a heartless world, to lift it up as a darkness that all may see, and for years I have practically failed. I have practically failed, but I am not without hope. I believe that my absurdity is at last beginning to obtain a meed of recognition. I believe that a few fine spirits are beginning to understand that artistic absurdity, the perfection of folly, has a bright and glorious future before it. I am absurd, and have been so for very many years, and in very many ways. I have been an æsthete. I have lain upon hearth-rugs and eaten passion-flowers. I have clothed myself in breeches of white samite, and offered my friends yellow jonquils instead of afternoon tea. But when æstheticism became popular in Bayswater—a part of London built for the delectation of the needy rich—I felt that it was absurd no longer, and I turned to other things. It was then, one golden summer day among the flowering woods of Richmond, that I invented a new art, the art of preposterous conversation. A middle-class country has prevented me from patenting my exquisite invention, which has been closely imitated by dozens of people much older and much stupider than myself; but nobody so far has been able to rival me in my own particular line of business, and my society 'turns' at luncheon parties, dances, and dinners are invariably received with an applause which is almost embarrassing, and which is scarcely necessary to one so admirably conceited as myself."

At this point, Esmé, whose face had been gradually assuming a pained and irritated expression, paused, and looking towards the west, which was barred with green and gold, and flecked with squadrons of rose-coloured cloudlets, exclaimed in a voice expressive of weakness—

"That sky is becoming so terribly imitative that I can hardly go on. Why are modern sunsets so intolerably true to Turner?"

He looked round as if for an answer; but, since nobody had anything to say, he passed one hand over his eyes, as if to shut out some dreadful vision, and continued with rather less vivacity—

"For the true artist is always conceited, just as the true Philistine is always fond of going to the Royal Academy. I have brought the art of preposterous conversation to the pitch of perfection; but I have been greatly handicapped in my efforts by the egregious wisdom of a world that insists upon taking me seriously. There is nothing that should be taken seriously, except, possibly, an income or the music halls, and I am not an income or a music hall, although I am intensely and strangely refined. Yet I have been taken seriously throughout my career. My lectures have been gravely discussed. My plays have been solemnly criticised by the amusing failures in literature who love to call themselves 'the gentlemen of the press.' My poems have been boycotted by prurient publishers; and my novel, 'The Soul of Bertie Brown,' has ruined the reputation of a magazine that had been successful in shocking the impious for centuries. Bishops have declared that I am a monster, and monsters have declared that I ought to be a bishop. And all this has befallen me because I am an artist in absurdity, a human being who dares to be ridiculous. I practise the exquisite art of folly, an art that will in the future take rank with the arts of painting, of music, of literature. I was born to be absurd. I have lived to be absurd. I shall die to be absurd; for nothing can be more absurd than the death of a man who has lived to sin, instead of having lived to suffer. I married to be absurd; for marriage is one of the most brilliant absurdities ever invented by a prolific imagination. We are all absurd; but we are not all artists, because we are not all self-conscious. The artist must be self-conscious. If we marry seriously, if we live solemnly, and die with a decent gravity, we are being absurd; but we do not know it, and therefore our absurdity has no value. I am an artist, because I am consciously absurd; and I wish to impress upon you to-day, that if you wish to live improperly, you must be consciously absurd too. You must commit follies; but you must not be under the impression that you are performing sensible acts, otherwise you will take rank with sensible people, who are invariably and hopelessly middle class."

An interruption occurred here—one of the smallest children who was stationed in the front of the group under the cedar tree suddenly bursting into a flood of tears, and having to be led, shrieking, away to a distant corner of the garden. Esmé followed its convulsed form with his eyes, and then remarked—

"That child is being absurd; but that child is not an artist, because it is not conscious of its absurdity. Remember, then, to be self-conscious, to set aside the normal, to be young, and to be eternally foolish. Take nothing seriously, except yourselves, if possible. Do not be deceived into thinking the mind greater than the face, or the soul grander than the body. Strike the words virtue and wickedness out of your dictionaries. There is nothing good and nothing evil. There is only art. Despise the normal, and flee from everything that is hallowed by custom, as you would flee from the seven deadly virtues. Cling to the abnormal. Shrink from the cold and freezing touch of Nature. One touch of Nature makes the whole world commonplace. Forget your Catechism, and remember the words of Flaubert and of Walter Pater, and remember this, too, that the folly of self-conscious fools is the only true wisdom! And now sing to us your hymn, sing to us under the cedar tree self-consciously, and we will listen self-consciously, even as Ulysses listened to—"

But here a gentle and penetrating "Hush!" broke from the lips of Mrs. Windsor, and Esmé paused.

"Sing to us," he said, "and we will listen as the old listen to the voices of youth, as the nightingale listens to the properly trained vocalist, as Nature listens to Art. Sing to us, beautiful rose-coloured children, until we forget that you are singing a hymn, and remember only that you are young, and that some day, in the long-delayed fulness of time, you will be no longer innocent."

He uttered the last words in a tone so soft and so seductive that it was like honey and the honeycomb, and then stood with his eyes fixed dreamily upon the children, who had been getting decidedly red and fidgety, unaccustomed to be directly addressed, and in so fantastic a manner. The relief of the teachers at the cessation of Amarinth's address was tumultuously obvious. They once more turned out their toes. The anguished expression died away from their faces, and they ceased to twist their fingers into curious patterns suggestive of freehand drawings. The national schoolmaster, unlocking his countenance, and delightedly assuming his wonted air of proud authority, stepped forward and called for the Old Hundredth; and in the gentle evening air the well-known tune ascended like incense to the darkening heavens. Shrilly the youthful voices rose and fell, until the amen came as a full stop. Then the little troop was marshalled two and two, made a collective obeisance to Mrs. Windsor and her guests, and wheeled out of the garden into the drive at a quick step, warbling poignantly, "Onward, Christian Soldiers." Gradually the sound decreased in volume, decreased in a long diminuendo, and at last faded away into silence.

Mrs. Windsor sighed.

"Children are very sticky," she remarked. "I am glad I never had any."

"Yes," said Madame Valtesi; "they are as adhesive as postage-stamps. What time do we dine to-day?"

"Not until half-past eight."

"I shall go in, and sit down quietly and try to feel old. Youth is quite terrible, in spite of what Esmé says. Esmé, youth is not passionate; it is merely sticky and excited."

"What a pity it is not self-consciously sticky," he murmured, accompanying her into the house.

"Why?"

"Then perhaps it might be induced to wash occasionally. I wonder if I can find a hock and seltzer. I feel like a volume of sermons—so very dry."

XV

T was a romantic evening, and although Lord Reggie prided himself on being altogether impervious to the influences of Nature, he was not unaware that a warm and fantastic twilight may incline the average woman favourably to a suit that she might not be disposed to heed in the early morning, or during the garish sunshine of a summer afternoon. He presumed that Lady Locke was an average woman, simply because he considered all women exceedingly and distinctively average; and therefore, when he saw a soft expression steal into her dark face as she glanced at the faded turquoise of the sky, he decided to propose at once, and as prettily as possible. But Tommy was fussing about, wavy with childish excitement, and at first he could not speak.

"Tommy," said Lady Locke at last, "give me a kiss and run away to your supper. But, before you go, listen to me. Did you attend to Mr. Amarinth's lecture?"

"Yes, yes, yes, mother! Of course, of course, of course!" cried Tommy, dancing violently on the lawn, and trying to excite Bung to a tempest.

"Well, remember that it was meant to be comic. It was only a nonsense lecture, like Edward Lear's nonsense books. Do you see? It was a turning of everything topsy-turvy. So what we have to do is just the opposite of everything Mr. Amarinth advised. You understand, my boy?"

"All right, mumsy," said Tommy. "But I forget what he said."

Lady Locke looked pleased, kissed his flushed little face, and packed him off.

"I hope the school children will do the same," she said to Lord Reggie when he was gone. "What a blessing a short memory can be!"

"Didn't you like the lecture, then?" Reggie asked. "I thought it splendid, so full of imagination, so exquisitely choice in language and in feeling."

"And so self-conscious."

"Yes, as all art must be."

"Art! art! You could make me hate that word!"

Reggie looked for once honestly shocked.

"You could hate art?" he said.

"Yes, if I could believe that it was the antagonist of Nature, instead of the faithful friend. No, I did not like the lecture, if one can like or dislike a mere absurdity. Tell me, Lord Reggie, are you self-consciously absurd?"

He drew his chair a little nearer to hers.

"I don't know," he said; "I hope I am beautiful. If I am beautiful, that is all I wish for. To be beautiful is to be complete. To be clever is easy enough. To be beautiful is so difficult, that even Byron had a club foot with all his genius. Cleverness can be acquired. Hundreds of stupid people nowadays acquire the faculty of cleverness. That is why society is so boring. You find people practising mental scales and five-finger exercises at every party you go to. The true artist will never practise. How soft this twilight is, though not so delicate and subtle as that in Millet's 'Angelus.' Lady Locke, I have something to tell you, and I will tell it to you now, while the stars come out, and the shadows steal from their homes in the trees. Esmé said to-day that marriage was a brilliant absurdity. Will you be brilliantly absurd? Will you marry me?"

He leaned forward, and took her hand rather negligently in his small and soft one. His face was calm, and he spoke in a clear and even voice. Lady Locke left her hand in his. She was quite calm too.

"I cannot marry you," she said. "Do you wish me to tell you why? Probably you do not; but I think I will tell you all the same. I am not brilliant, and therefore I have no wish to be absurd. If I married you I should be merely absurd without being brilliant at all. You do not love me. I think you love nothing. I like you; I am interested by you. Perhaps if you had a different nature I might even love you. But I can never love an echo, and you are an echo."

"An echo is often more beautiful than the voice it repeats," he said.

"But if the voice is quite ugly the echo cannot be beautiful," she answered. "I do not wish to be too frank, but as you have asked me to marry you I will say this. Your character seems to me to be an echo of Mr. Amarinth's. I believe that he merely poses; but do those who imitate him merely pose? Do you merely pose? What Mr.

Amarinth really is it is quite impossible to tell. Perhaps there is nothing real about him at all. Perhaps, as he has said, his real man is only a Mrs. Harris. He may be abnormal *au fond*; but you are not! What is your real self? Is it what I see, what I know?"

"Expression is my life," Lord Reggie said in a rather offended voice, drawing away his hand. A red spot appeared in each of his cheeks. He began to realise that he was refused because he was not admired. It seemed almost incredible.

"Then the expression that I see is you?" she asked.

"I suppose so," he replied, with a tinge of exceedingly boyish sulkiness.

"Then, till you have got rid of it never ask a woman to marry you. Men like you do not understand women. They do not try to; probably they could not if they did. Men like you are so twisted and distorted in mind that they cannot recognise their own distortion. It seems to me that Mr. Amarinth has created a cult. Let me call it the cult of the green carnation. I suppose it may be called modern. To me it seems very silly and rather wicked. If you would take that hideous green flower out of your coat, not because I asked you to, but because you hated it honestly, I might answer your question differently. If you could forget what you call art, if you could see life at all with a straight, untrammelled vision, if you could be like a man, instead of like nothing at all in heaven or earth except that dyed flower, I might perhaps care for you in the right way. But your mind is artificially coloured: it comes from the dyer's. It is a green carnation; and I want a natural blossom to wear in my heart."

She got up.

"You are not angry with me?" she asked.

Lord Reggie's face was scarlet.

"You talk very much like ordinary people," he said, a little rude in his hurt self-love.

"I am ordinary," she said. "I am so glad of it. I think that after this week I shall try to be even more ordinary than I already am."

Then she went slowly into the cottage.

That evening Lord Reggie told Mrs. Windsor that he found he must leave for town on the following morning.

She was horrified, and was still more appalled when Esmé Amarinth expressed an intention of accompanying him.

"It's worse than the Professor's fit last year," she said dolefully. "But perhaps it will be better if we all go back to town to-morrow.

You will not care to be rustic without any men, will you, Madame Valtesi?" she added.

"No," replied that lady. "It would be too much like having a bath in Tidman's salt, instead of in the ocean. It would be tame. We three women in this cottage together should be like the Graiæ, only we should not have even one eye and one tooth between us. Perhaps we have been rustic as long as is good for us. I shall go to the French plays to-morrow night. I like them—they always do me so much harm."

"And I will take Tommy to the seaside," said Lady Locke.

"My dear lady," said Esmé. "How terribly normal!"

"And how exceedingly healthy!" she replied.

He looked at her with a deep pity.

Next morning, as she bade good-bye to Lord Reggie, she said to him in a low voice—

"Some day, perhaps, you will throw away the green carnation."

"Oh! it will be out of fashion soon," he answered, as he got delicately into the carriage.

"So you have been refused, Reggie," said Esmé, as they drove towards the station. "How original you are! I should never have suspected you of that. But you were always wonderful—wonderful and very complete. When did you decide to be refused? Only last night. You managed it exquisitely. I think that I am glad. I do not want you to alter, and the refining influence of a really good woman is as corrosive as an acid. Ah, Reggie, you will not be singing in the woods near Esher when the tiresome cuckoo imitates Haydn's toy symphony next spring! You will still be living your marvellous scarlet life, still teaching the London tradesmen the exact value of your supreme aristocracy. If you had become a capitalist you might have grown whiskers and become respectable. Why do whiskers and respectability grow together? Here we are at the railway station. Railway stations always remind me of Mr. Terriss, the actor. They are so noisy. The Surrey week is over. Soon we shall see once more the tender grey of the Piccadilly pavement, and the subtle music of Old Bond Street will fall furtively upon our ears. Put your feet up on the opposite cushion, dear boy, while I lean out of the railway carriage window and smile the people away. When people try to get into my compartment I always smile at them, and they always go away. They think that I am mad. And are they mistaken? How can one tell? There is only one sanity in all the world, and that is to be artistically insane. Reggie, give me a gold-tipped cigarette, and I will be brilliant. I will be brilliant for you alone, remembering my Whistler as commonplace people remember their obligations, or as Madame Valtesi remembers to forget her birthday. Ah! we are off! Look out of this window, dear boy, and you will see two elderly gentlemen missing the train. They are doing it rather nicely. I think they must have been practising in private. There is an art even in missing a train, Reggie. But one of them is not quite perfect in it yet. He has begun to swear a little too soon!"

A CATALOGUE OF SELECTED DOVER BOOKS
IN ALL FIELDS OF INTEREST

A CATALOGUE OF SELECTED DOVER BOOKS
IN ALL FIELDS OF INTEREST

WHAT IS SCIENCE?, *N. Campbell*
The role of experiment and measurement, the function of mathematics, the nature of scientific laws, the difference between laws and theories, the limitations of science, and many similarly provocative topics are treated clearly and without technicalities by an eminent scientist. "Still an excellent introduction to scientific philosophy," H. Margenau in *Physics Today*. "A first-rate primer . . . deserves a wide audience," *Scientific American*. 192pp. 5⅜ x 8.
60043-2 Paperbound $1.25

THE NATURE OF LIGHT AND COLOUR IN THE OPEN AIR, *M. Minnaert*
Why are shadows sometimes blue, sometimes green, or other colors depending on the light and surroundings? What causes mirages? Why do multiple suns and moons appear in the sky? Professor Minnaert explains these unusual phenomena and hundreds of others in simple, easy-to-understand terms based on optical laws and the properties of light and color. No mathematics is required but artists, scientists, students, and everyone fascinated by these "tricks" of nature will find thousands of useful and amazing pieces of information. Hundreds of observational experiments are suggested which require no special equipment. 200 illustrations; 42 photos. xvi + 362pp. 5⅜ x 8.
20196-1 Paperbound $2.00

THE STRANGE STORY OF THE QUANTUM, AN ACCOUNT FOR THE GENERAL READER OF THE GROWTH OF IDEAS UNDERLYING OUR PRESENT ATOMIC KNOWLEDGE, *B. Hoffmann*
Presents lucidly and expertly, with barest amount of mathematics, the problems and theories which led to modern quantum physics. Dr. Hoffmann begins with the closing years of the 19th century, when certain trifling discrepancies were noticed, and with illuminating analogies and examples takes you through the brilliant concepts of Planck, Einstein, Pauli, Broglie, Bohr, Schroedinger, Heisenberg, Dirac, Sommerfeld, Feynman, etc. This edition includes a new, long postscript carrying the story through 1958. "Of the books attempting an account of the history and contents of our modern atomic physics which have come to my attention, this is the best," H. Margenau, Yale University, in *American Journal of Physics*. 32 tables and line illustrations. Index. 275pp. 5⅜ x 8.
20518-5 Paperbound $2.00

GREAT IDEAS OF MODERN MATHEMATICS: THEIR NATURE AND USE, *Jagjit Singh*
Reader with only high school math will understand main mathematical ideas of modern physics, astronomy, genetics, psychology, evolution, etc. better than many who use them as tools, but comprehend little of their basic structure. Author uses his wide knowledge of non-mathematical fields in brilliant exposition of differential equations, matrices, group theory, logic, statistics, problems of mathematical foundations, imaginary numbers, vectors, etc. Original publication. 2 appendixes. 2 indexes. 65 ills. 322pp. 5⅜ x 8.
20587-8 Paperbound $2.25

THE MUSIC OF THE SPHERES: THE MATERIAL UNIVERSE — FROM ATOM TO QUASAR, SIMPLY EXPLAINED, *Guy Murchie*
Vast compendium of fact, modern concept and theory, observed and calculated data, historical background guides intelligent layman through the material universe. Brilliant exposition of earth's construction, explanations for moon's craters, atmospheric components of Venus and Mars (with data from recent fly-by's), sun spots, sequences of star birth and death, neighboring galaxies, contributions of Galileo, Tycho Brahe, Kepler, etc.; and (Vol. 2) construction of the atom (describing newly discovered sigma and xi subatomic particles), theories of sound, color and light, space and time, including relativity theory, quantum theory, wave theory, probability theory, work of Newton, Maxwell, Faraday, Einstein, de Broglie, etc. "Best presentation yet offered to the intelligent general reader," *Saturday Review*. Revised (1967). Index. 319 illustrations by the author. Total of xx + 644pp. 5⅜ x 8½.
21809-0, 21810-4 Two volume set, paperbound $5.00

FOUR LECTURES ON RELATIVITY AND SPACE, *Charles Proteus Steinmetz*
Lecture series, given by great mathematician and electrical engineer, generally considered one of the best popular-level expositions of special and general relativity theories and related questions. Steinmetz translates complex mathematical reasoning into language accessible to laymen through analogy, example and comparison. Among topics covered are relativity of motion, location, time; of mass; acceleration; 4-dimensional time-space; geometry of the gravitational field; curvature and bending of space; non-Euclidean geometry. Index. 40 illustrations. x + 142pp. 5⅜ x 8½. 61771-8 Paperbound $1.35

HOW TO KNOW THE WILD FLOWERS, *Mrs. William Starr Dana*
Classic nature book that has introduced thousands to wonders of American wild flowers. Color-season principle of organization is easy to use, even by those with no botanical training, and the genial, refreshing discussions of history, folklore, uses of over 1,000 native and escape flowers, foliage plants are informative as well as fun to read. Over 170 full-page plates, collected from several editions, may be colored in to make permanent records of finds. Revised to conform with 1950 edition of Gray's Manual of Botany. xlii + 438pp. 5⅜ x 8½. 20332-8 Paperbound $2.50

MANUAL OF THE TREES OF NORTH AMERICA, *Charles Sprague Sargent*
Still unsurpassed as most comprehensive, reliable study of North American tree characteristics, precise locations and distribution. By dean of American dendrologists. Every tree native to U.S., Canada, Alaska; 185 genera, 717 species, described in detail—leaves, flowers, fruit, winterbuds, bark, wood, growth habits, etc. plus discussion of varieties and local variants, immaturity variations. Over 100 keys, including unusual 11-page analytical key to genera, aid in identification. 783 clear illustrations of flowers, fruit, leaves. An unmatched permanent reference work for all nature lovers. Second enlarged (1926) edition. Synopsis of families. Analytical key to genera. Glossary of technical terms. Index. 783 illustrations, 1 map. Total of 982pp. 5⅜ x 8.
20277-1, 20278-X Two volume set, paperbound $6.00

IT'S FUN TO MAKE THINGS FROM SCRAP MATERIALS,
Evelyn Glantz Hershoff
What use are empty spools, tin cans, bottle tops? What can be made from
rubber bands, clothes pins, paper clips, and buttons? This book provides
simply worded instructions and large diagrams showing you how to make
cookie cutters, toy trucks, paper turkeys, Halloween masks, telephone sets,
aprons, linoleum block- and spatter prints — in all 399 projects! Many are easy
enough for young children to figure out for themselves; some challenging
enough to entertain adults; all are remarkably ingenious ways to make things
from materials that cost pennies or less! Formerly "Scrap Fun for Everyone."
Index. 214 illustrations. 373pp. 5⅜ x 8½.   21251-3 Paperbound $1.75

SYMBOLIC LOGIC and THE GAME OF LOGIC, *Lewis Carroll*
"Symbolic Logic" is not concerned with modern symbolic logic, but is instead
a collection of over 380 problems posed with charm and imagination, using
the syllogism and a fascinating diagrammatic method of drawing conclusions.
In "The Game of Logic" Carroll's whimsical imagination devises a logical game
played with 2 diagrams and counters (included) to manipulate hundreds of
tricky syllogisms. The final section, "Hit or Miss" is a lagniappe of 101 addi-
tional puzzles in the delightful Carroll manner. Until this reprint edition,
both of these books were rarities costing up to $15 each. Symbolic Logic:
Index. xxxi + 199pp. The Game of Logic: 96pp. 2 vols. bound as one. 5⅜ x 8.
                                                                20492-8 Paperbound $2.50

MATHEMATICAL PUZZLES OF SAM LOYD, PART I
selected and edited by M. Gardner
Choice puzzles by the greatest American puzzle creator and innovator. Selected
from his famous collection, "Cyclopedia of Puzzles," they retain the unique
style and historical flavor of the originals. There are posers based on arithmetic,
algebra, probability, game theory, route tracing, topology, counter and sliding
block, operations research, geometrical dissection. Includes the famous "14-15"
puzzle which was a national craze, and his "Horse of a Different Color" which
sold millions of copies. 117 of his most ingenious puzzles in all. 120 line
drawings and diagrams. Solutions. Selected references. xx + 167pp. 5⅜ x 8.
                                                                20498-7 Paperbound $1.35

STRING FIGURES AND HOW TO MAKE THEM, *Caroline Furness Jayne*
107 string figures plus variations selected from the best primitive and modern
examples developed by Navajo, Apache, pygmies of Africa, Eskimo, in Europe,
Australia, China, etc. The most readily understandable, easy-to-follow book in
English on perennially popular recreation. Crystal-clear exposition; step-by-
step diagrams. Everyone from kindergarten children to adults looking for
unusual diversion will be endlessly amused. Index. Bibliography. Introduction
by A. C. Haddon. 17 full-page plates, 960 illustrations. xxiii + 401pp. 5⅜ x 8½.
                                                                20152-X Paperbound $2.25

PAPER FOLDING FOR BEGINNERS, *W. D. Murray and F. J. Rigney*
A delightful introduction to the varied and entertaining Japanese art of
origami (paper folding), with a full, crystal-clear text that anticipates every
difficulty; over 275 clearly labeled diagrams of all important stages in creation.
You get results at each stage, since complex figures are logically developed
from simpler ones. 43 different pieces are explained: sailboats, frogs, roosters,
etc. 6 photographic plates. 279 diagrams. 95pp. 5⅝ x 8⅜.
                                                                20713-7 Paperbound $1.00

THE WONDERFUL WIZARD OF OZ, *L. F. Baum*
All the original W. W. Denslow illustrations in full color—as much a part of "The Wizard" as Tenniel's drawings are of "Alice in Wonderland." "The Wizard" is still America's best-loved fairy tale, in which, as the author expresses it, "The wonderment and joy are retained and the heartaches and nightmares left out." Now today's young readers can enjoy every word and wonderful picture of the original book. New introduction by Martin Gardner. A Baum bibliography. 23 full-page color plates. viii + 268pp. 5⅜ x 8.
20691-2 Paperbound $1.95

THE MARVELOUS LAND OF OZ, *L. F. Baum*
This is the equally enchanting sequel to the "Wizard," continuing the adventures of the Scarecrow and the Tin Woodman. The hero this time is a little boy named Tip, and all the delightful Oz magic is still present. This is the Oz book with the Animated Saw-Horse, the Woggle-Bug, and Jack Pumpkinhead. All the original John R. Neill illustrations, 10 in full color. 287pp. 5⅜ x 8.
20692-0 Paperbound $1.75

ALICE'S ADVENTURES UNDER GROUND, *Lewis Carroll*
The original *Alice in Wonderland*, hand-lettered and illustrated by Carroll himself, and originally presented as a Christmas gift to a child-friend. Adults as well as children will enjoy this charming volume, reproduced faithfully in this Dover edition. While the story is essentially the same, there are slight changes, and Carroll's spritely drawings present an intriguing alternative to the famous Tenniel illustrations. One of the most popular books in Dover's catalogue. Introduction by Martin Gardner. 38 illustrations. 128pp. 5⅜ x 8½.
21482-6 Paperbound $1.00

THE NURSERY "ALICE," *Lewis Carroll*
While most of us consider *Alice in Wonderland* a story for children of all ages, Carroll himself felt it was beyond younger children. He therefore provided this simplified version, illustrated with the famous Tenniel drawings enlarged and colored in delicate tints, for children aged "from Nought to Five." Dover's edition of this now rare classic is a faithful copy of the 1889 printing, including 20 illustrations by Tenniel, and front and back covers reproduced in full color. Introduction by Martin Gardner. xxiii + 67pp. 6⅛ x 9¼.
21610-1 Paperbound $1.75

THE STORY OF KING ARTHUR AND HIS KNIGHTS, *Howard Pyle*
A fast-paced, exciting retelling of the best known Arthurian legends for young readers by one of America's best story tellers and illustrators. The sword Excalibur, wooing of Guinevere, Merlin and his downfall, adventures of Sir Pellias and Gawaine, and others. The pen and ink illustrations are vividly imagined and wonderfully drawn. 41 illustrations. xviii + 313pp. 6⅛ x 9¼.
21445-1 Paperbound $2.00

Prices subject to change without notice.

Available at your book dealer or write for free catalogue to Dept. Adsci, Dover Publications, Inc., 180 Varick St., N.Y., N.Y. 10014. Dover publishes more than 150 books each year on science, elementary and advanced mathematics, biology, music, art, literary history, social sciences and other areas.